Tyler Looked Into Jill's Eyes And Felt An Odd Tug Inside Him.

"I like the way your eyes shine in the moonlight."

Her lids slid downward, hiding her eyes from him. "Tyler," she said in a husky, sexy voice that felt like a stroke over key erogenous zones.

Glancing down, he noticed her sandal strap was twisted. He knelt down and untwisted it. He wrapped his hand around her ankle and rubbed his thumb over her smooth skin.

"You have small ankles, too," he said, skimming his hand up her calf, behind her knee to the inside of her thigh.

She stopped his wandering hand.

He met her gaze. "Does it bother you for me to touch you?"

"It's distracting," she said, her gaze smoky. "I know you're a flirt. You've succeeded in arousing—" she urged him upward and rested her hand on his chest "—my curiosity. But I want to know what's behind the flirt…."

Dear Reader,

Spring is in the air...and so is romance. Especially at Silhouette, where we're celebrating our 20th anniversary throughout 2000! And Silhouette Desire promises you six powerful, passionate, provocative love stories *every month.*

Fabulous Anne McAllister offers an irresistible MAN OF THE MONTH with *A Cowboy's Secret.* A rugged cowboy fears his darkest secret will separate him from the beauty he loves.

Bestselling author Leanne Banks continues her exciting miniseries LONE STAR FAMILIES: THE LOGANS with a sexy bachelor doctor in *The Doctor Wore Spurs.* In *A Whole Lot of Love,* Justine Davis tells the emotional story of a full-figured woman feeling worthy of love for the first time.

Kathryn Jensen returns to Desire with another wonderful fairy-tale romance, *The Earl Takes a Bride.* THE BABY BANK, a brand-new theme promotion in Desire in which love is found through sperm bank babies, debuts with *The Pregnant Virgin* by Anne Eames. And be sure to enjoy another BRIDAL BID story, which continues with Carol Devine's *Marriage for Sale,* in which the hero "buys" the heroine at auction.

We hope you plan to usher in the spring season with all six of these supersensual romances, only from Silhouette Desire!

Enjoy!

Joan Marlow Golan

Joan Marlow Golan
Senior Editor, Silhouette Desire

Please address questions and book requests to:
Silhouette Reader Service
U.S.: 3010 Walden Ave., P.O. Box 1325, Buffalo, NY 14269
Canadian: P.O. Box 609, Fort Erie, Ont. L2A 5X3

The Doctor Wore Spurs
LEANNE BANKS

Published by Silhouette Books
America's Publisher of Contemporary Romance

My gratitude to Millie Criswell
for the title and ten years of friendship.

This book is dedicated to all who have had the courage
to face their personal waterloo.

 SILHOUETTE BOOKS

ISBN 0-373-76280-1

THE DOCTOR WORE SPURS

Visit us at www.romance.net

Printed in U.S.A.

LEANNE BANKS

is a national number-one bestselling author of romance. She lives in her native Virginia with her husband and son and daughter. Recognized for both her sensual and humorous writing with two Career Achievement Awards from *Romantic Times Magazine,* Leanne likes creating a story with a few grins, a generous kick of sensuality and characters that hang around after the book is finished. Leanne believes romance readers are the best readers in the world because they understand that love is the greatest miracle of all. You can write to her at P.O. Box 1442, Midlothian, VA 23113. A SASE for a reply would be greatly appreciated.

*Four generations ago, the Logan family moved
west from Virginia and took a scrap of Texas land.
Despite droughts and floods, broken hearts and death,
the Logans now own one of the most successful
cattle ranches in Texas.*

*The Logans have power, brains and strength. Some
call their ongoing success a legacy. The Logans would
instead point to hard work, persistence and plain old
American ingenuity. When it comes to matters of the
heart, however, they refer to their inheritance as a curse.
The Logans face their greatest challenge in breaking
that curse, and finding a love that lasts forever....*

Prologue

"She has a reputation," Clarence Gilmore said, his gaze on the same woman Tyler Logan was watching.

Idly aware of the intense schmooze factor of the Hospital Association's convention, Tyler watched Jill Hershey the same way he'd been known to watch a buck during hunting season. The outer package was enough to merit a second glance: silky, warm-brown hair, intelligent green eyes and a compact but curvy body that was almost concealed by her conservative clothing. Another man might not notice the subtle swell of her breasts against the double-breasted black suit jacket or the enticing curve of her waist and hips, but Tyler always looked beneath the surface.

He just didn't always let everyone else know he did. What held his attention about Jill Hershey, however, was the way she kept her gaze focused on whomever she was talking to. Even from twenty feet away he could sense the power of her focus.

"What do you know about her?" he asked Clarence.

"She's a public relations miracle worker. That's why she's in demand. You wouldn't believe what she did for the cancer treatment center in Minneapolis," Clarence, the hospital administrator, said wistfully.

"Then get her," Tyler said simply.

Clarence threw him a long-suffering glance. "You surgeons don't understand anything about the business of health care."

"Good thing, too," Tyler said with a grin. "We'd have a lot more dead people, if surgeons were thinking about business instead of surgery." He looked at Jill again. "If she's the one we need to beef up our children's treatment center, then get her."

"There might be a few obstacles to that. One, she probably costs too much. Two, she's probably already booked. Three, we might be too small."

"Sounds like a bunch of mights and maybes. What's the harm in asking?"

"I've requested information about her before," Clarence said a shade defensively. "I was told she doesn't do children's projects."

That stopped Tyler. He glanced at Clarence. "Really?"

"Yes," Clarence said, pulling slightly on his collar.

"Well, maybe she needs a new challenge," Tyler said.

"You're not going to approach her," Clarence said.

"Sure I am. Isn't that why we're at this convention? To gain some visibility for the new children's cardiac wing."

"Yes, but—"

Tyler shrugged. "You said she's the one we need. So, I'll go get her."

The man with the cowboy hat waited patiently behind her former client, Mr. Waldron. Jill tried not to look at him, but it was difficult. He was taller than most men in the room, unabashedly Western, and, she concluded after a few moments passed, determined. He was a little too handsome for his own good, she thought. Just the way he stood, he exuded a gut-level kind of confidence most people never experienced. His searching gaze generated an odd ripple inside her.

Her former client must have felt the man's presence because he glanced around quizzically.

The man immediately stepped forward. "Hello, I'm Dr. Tyler Logan from Fort Worth General Hospital. Pleased to meet you."

"Bill Waldron of Cincinnati University Hospital. This is—"

"Jill Hershey, public relations sorceress," Dr. Logan finished with enigmatic charm. He extended his hand and met her gaze with the direct impact of a two-by-four. "We need you."

Jill blinked. Although her career success had grown quickly over the past three years, she wasn't accustomed to this approach. Noticing the strength and size of his hand, she managed a smile. "I'm flattered," she said. "I think."

Mr. Waldron excused himself, and Jill retrieved her hand. "I wouldn't call myself a sorceress."

"You don't have to. You have others who do it for you."

She felt a surge of curiosity. She wondered what was behind his cowboy charm. "Dr. Logan," she began.

"Call me Tyler," he said.

Surprise seeped through her. Many of the doctors she'd met were very attached to their titles. "Tyler, what is your specialty?"

"Pediatric cardiology. Surgery."

Jill's stomach clenched. It took a moment to catch her breath, but with effort she produced a smile. "That's an important field, but I must tell you I haven't done much work with children's projects."

"Why not?"

His question took her off guard. "I always felt I was more effective with other specialties."

"You don't like kids?"

"No!" she immediately denied, and shook her head. "I...I do like children." She shrugged, wanting to get away from this impertinent man who had unknowingly stabbed her in her most vulnerable area. "I told you I have always felt I was more effective with other specialties. Not only that," she said, wishing her voice didn't sound so tight with tension, "my latest projects have been with larger hospitals."

"You wouldn't want to get in a rut," Tyler said.

Jill's head began to pound. "A rut?" she repeated.

He nodded. "You look like a woman who needs a new challenge to keep you happy."

She didn't know what irritated her more, the fact that he was making a huge assumption or the fact that it was right. "Dr. Logan—"

"Tyler," he corrected, his blue eyes glinting with masculine humor.

She stifled a sigh. "Tyler, I have to be honest. I usually accept assignments recommended by the president of my company. If you're interested in our services, you can contact Jordan Grant. Our telephone and fax numbers are in the conference kit. It was nice meeting you."

He nodded slowly, thoughtfully, as if he saw more than she wanted him to see. Jill turned away, both disturbed and relieved.

"I dare you," she heard from behind her. His words brought her back around.

"Pardon?"

"I dare you to come to Fort Worth General and make a lot of children's lives longer and better. You've got what it takes to do it." He looked her directly in the eye, and she felt the heat and power of his passion. "I dare you."

One

Jill could hold her own. She'd had years of practice, and she rarely played the fool. She was no coward, and she knew how to protect herself. The first week after Dr. Tyler Logan had audaciously delivered his challenge, she'd dismissed him and his hospital. She refused to be manipulated.

As much as she dismissed him, however, he kept popping up. He'd had no idea of the enormity of his dare. He'd had no idea that he was presenting her with the opportunity to conquer or be conquered by her greatest, most secret pain.

And that was why she was currently organizing her temporary office at Fort Worth General Hospital. She glanced out her window at "Cowtown's" downtown area. A few blocks away stood the old stockyards, a statue of the legendary cowboy William Pickett, and Billy Bob's bar, the largest saloon in Texas. Wherever Jill's projects took her, she'd learned her job went much easier if she understood the natives. That meant she was going to have to be a temporary cowgirl. That might be challenging, considering she didn't eat beef.

"It's just temporary," she whispered, trying to settle her nervous stomach. "Temporary insanity." During her stay in Fort Worth, this office would be her safe haven, the place where she could close the door and take deep breaths, her island of peace and creativity. Her sanctuary.

A sharp rap sounded on her door, then it whooshed open. "Welcome to Cowtown."

Jill's stomach tightened again. That voice had haunted her during the past month. The man wasn't important, she reminded herself. He was merely a door she would walk through to make peace with herself. She glanced up to meet his blue gaze. The incongruous combination of his white coat, a stethoscope with a tiny stuffed bear attached to it and his cowboy hat caught her off guard. Even though the man was tall with broad shoulders and dark good looks, that tiny stuffed bear should have deep-sixed his sexual appeal. It didn't. "Thank you," she finally said.

"What took you so long to get here?"

She gave a light laugh and relaxed slightly. "You were that sure I'd come."

"If you followed your instincts," he said, entering the room. "You'll like it here."

"It's temporary," she said more for herself than him.

"You didn't answer my question. What took you so long?"

That Texas drawl and lanky stride were deceptive, Jill thought, hiding a grin. The man was impatient. Jill understood impatience. She'd just learned to conceal hers. "This may surprise you, but I was working on another project at the time. I needed to tie up some loose ends and make sure there was a smooth transition between me and the new rep. I couldn't just snap my fingers."

"Well, I *am* surprised," Tyler said. "You're supposed to be a sorceress, remember?"

She shot him a sideways glance. "I'm curious," she said. "Is this how you usually get your way with people?"

He picked up a pencil holder. "How?"

"Oh, by using a combination of flattery and manipulation."

He widened his eyes in mock innocence. "Flattery?" He shrugged. "I just tell the truth. And manipulation sounds mean. I'm not mean. I just do what it takes to get the job done. That makes some people nervous. What about you?"

"What about me?"

"Do I make you nervous?" he asked in a voice like black velvet.

Her heart jumped in her chest. "No," she said, a half beat more quickly than she should.

"Good," he said, "because you and I will be working together. I make the administration a little jumpy sometimes, but I get the job done." His lips twitched. "You're here, aren't you?"

"Temporarily," she emphasized.

His gaze swept over her. "Long enough," he promised. "Why are you staring at Wild Cody?"

Jill blinked. "Wild Cody?"

"My bear. You remind me of one of my kids."

She felt her cheeks heat. "I'm not used to seeing a bear on a stethoscope."

"Distracting, isn't it?" His lips twitched again when she nodded. "That's the idea." He took her hand and held it in his, then took her index finger between his fingers.

Feeling a strange, tumbling sensation in her stomach, she tried to pull back.

Tyler shook his head. "Hold on." He pulled another tiny bear from his pocket and attached the little bear to her finger. "You are now officially a member of the heart menders' wild posse."

Why was her heart pounding? she wondered with a kick of exasperation. She glanced at the little stuffed bear and sighed. Oddly touched, she smiled. "Thank you. Do you give these to your patients?"

He raised his eyebrows. "That's not a bad idea.

Maybe I could get them in bulk. I can see Clarence twitching over a purchase requisition for a hundred miniature bears.'' He grinned and squeezed her hand. ''There you go. A good idea and you haven't even been here an entire day. I told you we needed you.''

Her stomach turned another somersault. ''Ideas are the easy part. The hard part comes later,'' she murmured, thinking he had no idea how hard this could become for her.

''You need a challenge,'' he told her.

His assumption nettled her again. ''Why do you say that? You don't even know me.''

''I could say your reputation precedes you,'' he said. ''Or I could say we needed you at Fort Worth General because you've got great legs. Or I could just say I know a kindred spirit when I see one.''

''Is this a multiple-choice quiz?'' she asked, her voice betraying her impatience.

He leaned closer and she could see the very devil in his blue eyes. ''Check all of the above.''

A flirt, she concluded with disapproval. Her ex-husband had been charming, too confident and an outrageous flirt. She didn't need to read that book again. ''I don't think—''

''Howdy!'' a young, plump woman called from the doorway. Her gaze immediately latched on to Tyler. ''Oh, hi, Dr. Logan,'' she said in a breathy voice.

"Hi, Trina," Tyler said. "This is our PR specialist, Jill Hershey."

Her gaze weaving between Tyler and Jill, she said, "I'm Trina Hostetter and I'll be your assistant while you're here in Fort Worth."

"Good job," Tyler said as he moved toward the door. "Trina, you take good care of Jill. She's going to do great things for us." His gaze dipped to Jill's legs for an audacious extra second, then he gave a half grin. "See you later."

Jill watched Trina gaze longingly after Tyler. "I'd like to do great things for *him*," Trina murmured under his breath.

Jill rolled her eyes. "He's a flirt."

Trina swerved her head around. "But not a mean flirt," she quickly said. "He just knows how to make a woman feel good. He doesn't break hearts."

Jill raised her eyebrows doubtfully, but smiled. "Why do I think you might be a little prejudiced?"

"Oh. Just because it's obvious that I'd like Tyler to park his boots under my bed anytime, you think I might be prejudiced." Trina shook her head. "Just about every woman with any taste would like to have Tyler. What's not to like? He's handsome, but not pretty. He's smart, funny, kind, and he likes kids. Sure, he dates a lot, but he doesn't make promises he won't keep. Everyone's just trying to find a way to get him to make some of those promises." She glanced at Jill's finger. "Omigod, he gave you

one of his bears. He must really like you," she said
with a trace of envy.

Jill immediately unfastened the bear from her finger and transferred it to a pencil. "Don't worry. It
has no romantic significance. The reason Tyler
wants me here is because he believes I'm going to
help him get something he wants—the new pediatric
cardiology wing."

Trina blinked. "Are you saying you don't want
him?"

Jill smiled. "Exactly. I would rather catch the flu
than catch Tyler."

"Are you married? Engaged?"

"No, just sane. Very sane when it comes to men.
Believe me," Jill said, feeling a rumbling of trepi-
dation inside her. "I'm not here to get involved with
Dr. Logan."

A sharp rap sounded on Jill's office door, startling
her and breaking her concentration. The door
opened and Tyler strode in. "Time for your tour,"
he said.

Jill blinked in irritation. The man always seemed
to catch her off guard. "Trina already took me on
a tour of the hospital," Jill told him. Trina had also
given her an earful on just about every person
they'd encountered.

"That was Trina's tour. Mine is different."

"Trina was very thorough," Jill said.

"I'm sure she was," Tyler said with a dry

chuckle. "You probably felt like you'd walked through scripts for three soap operas by the time she finished."

"It was—" she paused and her lips twitched "—colorful."

"I can tell you're in PR. My tour is different," he said. "I want you to meet some of my patients."

Jill's stomach tightened. "Oh, well, you don't have to do that."

He met her gaze. "Sure I do. People put more on the line when it's personal. If you meet some of these kids, it will be personal."

She nodded slowly. "You're right, but we don't have to do it today. I'm sure you've had a long day, and I'm digesting all the information I've gathered today and—"

"Why don't you want to meet them?"

Her breath stopped somewhere between her lungs and her mouth. How could she tell him that she wasn't prepared to face her demons in that way today? She couldn't. She carefully inhaled and exhaled. "I didn't say I don't want to meet them. I just thought there might be a better day."

"Nope," he said with a shrug.

She bit her lip and nodded. "Okay," she said, resignation sinking into her as she walked out of her office with him.

"We have three recovering from surgery and four either in for testing or preparing for surgery," he said as he led her with his long-legged stride through the white-tile corridor to the elevator.

"What age?" she asked, telling herself she could handle this.

"Infant through teenage."

Infant. Jill steeled herself against the poke at her secret wound. Focus on something else, she told herself. "What made you choose your specialty?"

He nodded for her to enter the elevator. "I think it chose me. If my father had chosen, he would've kept me on the ranch. Thank goodness my oldest brother is the rancher."

"Sounds like your family is big on tradition."

He shrugged. "You could say that. We've been around West Texas for several generations now, we have a long-standing feud with our neighbor, and some say there's a curse on the Logan name."

"A curse?" she echoed, intrigued at the prospect that the cocky, charming Dr. Logan could suffer from a curse.

He rolled his eyes. "I never believed it, but the Logans have not been particularly lucky in the romance department. Their women don't seem to hang around."

"They leave?"

He shrugged again. "Or die."

Her eyes widened and she swallowed a chuckle. "Oh, my. Is that why you haven't married?"

He shoved his hands in his pockets. "Nah, just

haven't met the right one." He looked her over curiously. "What about you?"

"I thought I had, but I was wrong."

"I thought someone would have tried to take you off the market. What did he do?"

"He left at the worst possible moment," she said and smiled. "No fairy-tale ending, but I'm over it now."

"Ready to go again?" he asked with a flicker of sexual challenge in his blue eyes.

"I like taking my time," she returned, thinking he would be a tempting package for some other woman. She met his gaze. "I know it's part of your style to flirt with women and to flatter. You don't have to do that with me. My ego can handle the direct approach."

He glanced at her mouth, then back to her eyes, and he gave a sensual grin. "What if I like flirting with you?"

"I think you should save it for the legions of women around here who want to—" she paused, then added Trina's words "—lasso your heart."

He roared with laughter. "You've been talking to Trina."

"No. Trina's been talking to me."

"So you're not gonna try to lasso me," he said, rubbing his chin. "I wonder if my feelings should be hurt."

"I'm sure you'll survive," she said in a dry voice. "No ropes, no chains. If I want your body or your face, it'll be for a media photo op that will get you your new wing.''

''Some men might see that as a challenge,'' he told her.

''I'm glad you're too intelligent for that,'' she said with far more assurance than she felt. Intelligence was one thing, the male ego another.

The elevator stopped. ''We'll see,'' he said. ''But right now you get to meet some of my kids. Hey, Betty,'' he called to a nurse. ''How's TJ?''

''A little down. His mom might not be here until tomorrow morning.''

Tyler winced and swore under his breath. ''TJ is seven and has six brothers and sisters. His family lives three hours away and his dad has a broken leg, so his mother is doing triple duty right now. He has surgery tomorrow to repair a hole in his heart. This is his room.''

''Hey, bud,'' he said as he entered the room. ''What's up?''

TJ was thin, his face drawn and his eyes frightened. Jill's heart immediately went out to him.

''My mom won't be here until late tonight.''

''I heard,'' Tyler said. ''I'm sure she'll be here as soon as she can. I need you to rest for surgery tomorrow.''

''Will I really be able to play baseball after the operation?''

''No reason from my end. Who knows? After you recover, the majors may be calling you.''

TJ smiled.

"Hey, I brought someone to meet you. Her name is Jill Hershey."

"Hershey?" TJ repeated. "Like the candy?"

"Yeah, eye candy," Tyler said and winked at her. "Like the kiss."

"Is she your girlfriend?"

"No," Jill quickly said. "I work at the hospital."

TJ glanced at her street clothes in confusion. "You're not gonna take any more of my blood or give me any more shots, are you?"

"Not me," she assured him. "Dr. Logan tells me you have a lot of brothers and sisters. Are you the oldest?"

TJ shook his head. "I'm in the middle. I had to come early for surgery because one of my sisters got sick and they didn't want me to get sick before the operation."

"Oh," Jill said. "It can be boring in the hospital."

"Yeah."

"Boring?" Tyler repeated indignantly. "Them's fighting words."

"Well, you get to do the interesting stuff like surgery," Jill pointed out.

"And TJ gets to lie around and have people wait on him."

"The food is gross," TJ said.

"What do you like to do at home?" Jill asked.

"After I get my operation, I'm gonna run and run

and never stop running,'' TJ said, his words pulling at Jill's heart. She could tell that was a dream Tyler would make come true. "I read a lot," he said. "My mom reads to all of us every night."

Jill glanced at the stack of books on his bedside stand. "Would you let me read one to you?"

TJ's eyes lit up. "Sure!"

Jill felt Tyler's hand on her shoulder. "You—" His pager went off and he glanced at it. "Another doctor. Probably needs a consult." He looked at her with a mixture of approval and basic male interest that made her heart jump and her brain go *uh-oh*. "I'll be back."

Jill didn't really want to like Tyler, but she was hard-pressed when she looked at TJ and knew he probably dreamed every night of running, and Tyler would make that dream a reality. Good press, she thought, and tried to compartmentalize as she picked up a book from the table.

Jill read several books to TJ, and much later Tyler appeared and removed the book she was currently reading from her hands. He pressed his finger to his lips and pointed at TJ, who was sleeping.

Taking her hand, he led her from the room. "I didn't intend to put you to work tonight."

She let go of his hand and waved hers in a dismissing gesture. "It was a small thing. I didn't mind at all."

He paused, studying her. "I think there's more to you than meets the eye. You look cool, as if you are totally pulled together, as if no one could ruffle your feathers or get to you,'' he said. ''But TJ did. I thought you didn't like kids.''

Jill stifled a sigh of frustration. ''I never said I didn't like kids. I just said I've been most effective working on projects for adults,'' she said, then changed the subject. ''How was your consult?''

''Two consults, and I checked in on another patient. That's what took me so long. There's one more thing I want you to see,'' he said, and touched her back to guide her toward the elevator. ''One floor up, then I'll take you to dinner.''

''Dinner's not necessary,'' Jill said.

''Sure it is.''

''No it isn't.''

''Sure it is,'' he repeated. ''Haven't you ever heard you're not supposed to argue with the doctor?''

''Is that one of the bits of fiction they teach you in med school?'' she asked sweetly.

Tyler chuckled. ''No respect. I get no respect.'' The doors whisked open. ''I can't let you read to her,'' he said as they rounded a corner, ''but I thought you might like to see my youngest patient.'' They stopped in front of a nursery window, and he pointed to a small baby off to the side. ''Meet Annabelle Rogers. She's three months old.''

Jill saw the nursery full of isolates with babies wrapped in blankets, and she broke into a cold sweat. The image of another hospital and another nursery swam before her eyes. Tyler was talking, but she couldn't hear him. Instead, she heard another doctor's voice from another time.

"I'm sorry, Mrs. Hershey. We could not save your baby."

The words echoed in her head, and everything went black.

Two

Tyler caught Jill as her body slumped in a faint. He swore under his breath. The woman was white as a sheet.

"Mr. Logan, do you have to do that in the hall?" an anesthesiologist, Bill Johnson, joked as he passed by. "Can't you use the laundry closet like everyone else?"

Comedians. He was surrounded by comedians. "She fainted," he said.

Bill's eyes widened and he stopped. "Well, I guess she picked the right place. Let's get her feet elevated. Oxygen."

"No need," Tyler said, watching Jill's eyes flutter.

"She's pretty. I haven't seen her around. Who is she?"

"PR consultant," Tyler said, moving toward an empty room. "She's helping get the new wing."

"Smart, too. Hey, you want me to carry her?"

Tyler knew Bill was a player with the women. He felt a wave of protection for Jill as he set her down on the bed. "Keep your paws off her. This isn't your specialty. You like to put people to sleep, remember."

"Yes, but I also wake them up," he said, poking out his chest.

"Hey, candy lady, where'd you go?" Tyler asked, and slid his stethoscope against her chest.

Jill blinked. "I don't know. I just saw the—" Her slim eyebrows furrowed slightly and she looked away. "Maybe I was more tired than I thought. I never faint. I have never fainted in my life."

"What did you eat for lunch?"

"A pack of crackers, but—"

Tyler frowned. "You need some food."

"I'll get you a burger," Bill offered, stepping forward. "I'd like a rain check to take you someplace nicer when you're feeling better, but—"

"Not in this century," Tyler said, and sighed. "This is Dr. Bill Johnson. He puts people to sleep for a living."

Bill scowled. "Not women."

"He's worse than I am." He turned to Bill. "She doesn't like flirts, Bill."

"I'm not a flirt," Bill said, his gaze fixed on Jill with the intensity of a hunter. "I am a man. At your service," he added smoothly. "May I get you a burger?"

Tyler thought he might puke.

"Not unless it's a veggie burger," Jill said with a wry smile. "I don't really eat beef."

Tyler and Bill stared at each other, then roared with laughter.

"I missed the joke," Jill said, sitting up.

"Your secret is safe with us, but since you're in PR, you might want to remember you're in Texas," Tyler said. "Beef country."

"You're saying the Texas Rangers might come after me if I eat a veggie burger?"

"More likely the Cattlemen's Association," Bill said.

"Is a grilled cheese okay?"

"Done," Bill said, and gave Tyler a competitor's smile. "And you'd probably rather get a ride home with me, since Tyler drives a motorcycle."

"The fresh air will do her good," Tyler said.

"I can drive myself," Jill said.

"No," Tyler said at the same time Bill did. "Go get her grilled cheese," he growled.

Forty-five minutes later she had eaten and was pacing the floor of his office. She batted his hands away when he lifted his stethoscope. "Leave me alone. I'm ready to go."

"Okay, let's get your coat." He ditched his coat and grabbed his suede jacket.

"I really can drive myself," she said firmly.

"There is no way in hell I'm letting you," he said just as firmly. "And I'm bigger than you are, so just stop arguing."

She made a sound of disgust and stomped out of his office. Tyler's lips twitched. She was a strange combination. She looked so feminine and composed, a little too cool, as if nothing would shake her, but he'd watched her melt with TJ, and she was clearly embarrassed that she'd fainted. She looked as though she should be shaken and stirred, and he wouldn't mind doing the job. He knew she wouldn't take him too seriously, and that made her all the more appealing.

He escorted her to his bike in the parking lot, and she shook her head. "I'm not dressed for this."

Idly noticing the mild temperature and starry night, he pulled a helmet onto his head. "You're fine. You're staying at the Winchester Condominiums, aren't you?"

"Yes, but—"

He stopped her protest by putting a helmet on her head. "It's not far," he said with a grin. "Just hold on tight."

He helped her onto the motorcycle, then slid in front of her. He felt her gingerly put her hands on his back. Tyler pulled her slender hands under his coat and pressed them to his chest. "Trust me," he said. "You'll stay warmer this way."

He felt the inside of her thighs spreading to accommodate his rear end, and a sensual image pulsed through him. Jill, with her silky thighs spreading to accommodate him in a totally different way. He felt a rush of heat and sucked in a breath of air. Then he started the engine.

He drove through the night to her condominium and helped her off the bike. She fumbled with the helmet and he took it off for her. He couldn't explain it, but there was a hint of lost-girl look in her eyes. He'd seen flashes of that same look several times throughout the evening and he wondered what or who had caused it.

"Let me walk you to your door," he said.

"That's not—"

"Don't waste your breath. My mother would never forgive me."

"You can tell her I excused you," Jill said in a long-suffering voice.

Tyler smiled and shook his head. "Not unless we're planning to hold a séance."

Jill whipped her head around to stare at him. "She's dead?"

He nodded.

"I'm sorry. How long?"

"Too long," he said, remembering the woman who had personified gentleness, humor and love in his life. "She died twenty-three years ago when my sister, Martina, was born."

Jill stopped midstep on the sidewalk and placed her hand on his arm. "During childbirth. How terrible for all of you. Your sister, Martina? Did she survive?"

He nodded. "Yeah, and she's pregnant. Not married," he admitted with a sigh. "Whenever my brother and I ask her about the father, and believe me that is often, she insists the stork is responsible."

"Do you worry about her?"

"Yes," he said. "And no. Martina is no fragile flower. She's tough, and she knows if she needs anything, anything at all, she can call Brock or me and we'll come running."

"Lucky lady?" she asked, walking to her doorstep.

"Maybe," he said and cracked a half grin. "She might disagree with that on occasion."

She slid her hand through her hair and met his gaze. "Thank you."

"For catching you when you fell."

She paused a moment, then nodded. "Yes. You were kind. Pushy," she said, her lips tilting in a smile, "but kind."

"Yeah, but my pushy is better than Bill's pushy." She looked bone weary. "What are you going to do now?"

"Turn my sound machine to ocean waves and head for the Mexican Riviera."

"Take your rest. You earned it," Tyler said. "You did some heart mending tonight with TJ."

She shook her head and shrugged. "All I did was read to him."

He lifted his hand to her cheek. "You know it was more. Maybe you weren't heart mending. Heart stealing."

She gave him a sideways glance. "I thought we'd decided you didn't need to flirt with me."

He chuckled, liking the softness of her skin against his fingers. "Your hair is perfect, your clothes classic. You look like a cool, controlled lady who knows exactly how to rule her world. I don't know if I can resist the urge to mess your hair and rock your world."

She dipped her head slightly, and her eyes, well, her eyes dared the devil in him. "Try," she said, and left him staring at her door.

Jill leaned against the door and let the dark quiet of the condo seep into her. It would have been nice to be held right now. It would have been nice to feel strong arms around her and to hear reassuring words. A high-impact visual of Tyler flashed through her mind, and she tried to shake it off. He was tempting. He shouldn't be, but he was.

She remembered the strength of his body during the short ride from the hospital, and the combination of fire and gentleness in his blue eyes. He was the kind of man who never let a woman forget she was a woman and he was a man.

In a weak moment, when her defenses were lowered, she could be susceptible.

She shook her head and pushed away his image. She took a few slow, deep breaths to clear the noise from her mind and waited for the other images she'd run from during the past four years....

Seven months pregnant, she'd been certain she looked like a beached whale, but she'd been too excited to care. Her baby was due in two months, and every kick she felt inside her made her smile. The ultrasound had revealed she was growing a boy; he was so active she'd called him "grasshopper." Her husband of one year was eagerly anticipating their baby, too. The nursery was ready, she'd scheduled a long maternity leave, and she had never felt more complete in her life.

It was winter, and on her way home from work she drove the busy, slippery northern Virginia route with extra caution. When the truck careened over the median, headed directly for her, there was nowhere to go and nothing she could do.

Hours later she had awakened in the hospital. She remembered touching her stomach waiting for the kick of her baby inside her. She remembered how the anesthesia couldn't dull the slice of fear and pain. Grasshopper. She must have cried out. The nurse and doctor came to her side, and she heard the fateful words. "I'm sorry, Mrs. Hershey. We did everything we could, but we couldn't save your baby. He was too young and lost too much blood.''

Jill had never felt so empty in her life. She cried like a child. She wanted to run home, to run away from her pain, but she had been too seriously injured, she was told. She had lost too much blood and had almost died, too. There were more than a few moments she'd wished she had died.

Her husband was remote. Jill blamed herself. She suspected her husband blamed her, too. If only she had left five minutes earlier. Or five minutes later. If only.

Jill felt the salty moisture from her eyes stream down her cheeks. She slid her hands down to her flat belly and remembered Grasshopper's kick. The memory and the pain were different than she'd expected, perhaps sweeter because of the passing of time. Jill took a deep breath. Maybe the anticipation had been worse than the reality.

But *fainting?* She swiped her cheeks and rolled her eyes. She hadn't fared well on her first test here in Fort Worth. She smiled wryly thinking, in that case, she had nowhere to go but up.

The following morning Jill took her sound machine and kava tea with her to the hospital. The goal was to surround herself with comfort to encourage creativity and peace.

Trina looked at her, perplexed. ''Are you sure you don't want a honey bun and some good strong coffee? Dr. Logan told me to make sure you get plenty of food today."

Jill smiled. "Thank you. I already ate cereal."

"But a midmorning snack—"

"Okay," she said, sensing surrender would work better than protest. "I'll eat a honey bun." Comfort food, she told herself.

Trina sighed in relief. "Good. I don't want Dr. Logan mad at me. Have you ever seen a doctor with a better backside?"

"I can't say I've noticed his backside," Jill said wryly, which wasn't exactly true. She'd been up close and personal with Tyler's legs and backside when she'd ridden home on his motorcycle.

"Well, it's pretty darn terrific," Trina said. "And if he smiles and squints his eyes at the same time, he gets a little dimple right here," she said, pointing to the hollow of her jaw.

Jill tapped her pencil on her desk. If she heard much more about how wonderful Tyler was, she might be too nauseated to finish the honey bun. In Trina's eyes, the man was nearly a god, certainly a hero. That thought stopped her, then her mind tumbled through a half-dozen scenarios.

"I'm bugging you, aren't I?"

"No. You might be helping," Jill said. "I'm just thinking of ways to get the wing." She pinched a piece off the honey bun and put it in her mouth. "Maybe…" She closed her eyes, then opened them and smiled at her idea. "I've got it. An ad campaign featuring Tyler. We could take pictures in his scrubs and in his white jacket and invite people to donate funds to become members of Tyler's heart menders' posse.''

"Bumper stickers," Trina said.

"Yes. Great," Jill said. "I'd like you to call the on-site PR coordinator so I can bounce this off her as soon as possible and arrange for a photographer.''

Trina nodded. "And do you want me to call Dr. Logan, too?''

Jill shook her head. "Not until I take care of the groundwork.''

"But what if he won't do it?'' Trina asked. "Some men, even good-looking men are funny about getting their picture taken.''

Jill chuckled. Tyler's picture wasn't just going to be taken. If she had her way, the campaign would be plastered across all the local media along with a few billboards. "I don't think we'll have a problem with Tyler." She thought about his Texas-size ego. "He'll like this.''

"I don't like this," Tyler said late that afternoon when Jill told him her plan.

She did a double take. "Why? You're handsome and appealing. I'm sure the camera will love you as will everyone who sees your pictures. We'll get the funding for the wing in no time and you'll probably get a few hundred decent and indecent proposals, too. You'll be a hometown hero.''

He supposed he could feel flattered that Jill thought he was handsome. He wouldn't mind her stroking more than his ego. At the moment, however, he felt more like a prize bull being readied for a parade around the stockyard. Uneasy, Tyler shoved his hands in his pockets. "I'm not celebrity material."

She cocked her head to one side, her eyes glinting with a curiosity that grabbed at his gut and shimmied down. "Don't sell yourself short. Besides, this will be temporary."

"Five minutes?" he asked dryly.

She smiled gently. "Two weeks intensive, two more weeks of follow-up."

Tyler stifled an oath. "Don't you have any other ideas?"

Her face puzzled, Jill stood. "Yes, but this one is the best."

"This sounds an awful lot like that stupid bachelor calendar the Daughters of Texas put together every year," he grumbled. "I hear most of the guys don't wear much more than briefs and oil."

Jill chuckled, then bit her lip as if she sensed he wasn't amused. "You'll be wearing the clothes you wear to work. I must confess oil had not entered my mind."

He scratched his jaw. "I like my privacy. I'm not cut out to be a poster boy. All I want is to do my surgery, take care of my patients and lead my life the way I want. If I'd wanted a lot of attention, I would've chosen the rodeo.''

Jill shook her head. "I would have sworn you would do just about anything for this wing.''

He thought about the wing: how important it was to him and how important it would be to the patients. "I would,'' he said slowly, the words torn from him. "If it's absolutely necessary,'' he added. "I'm surprised you want me to do the media. I'm not the most politically correct guy in the corral. Have you talked with Clarence?''

"No, but you don't need to be totally politically correct. You're passionate about what you do. With very little coaching, that passion will come through.''

Feeling trapped, Tyler swiped his hand over his face. "My brother will never let me live this down. What in hell made you come up with this idea?''

Her smooth, composed expression faltered, and her cheeks bloomed with color. "Just a side remark Trina made. It doesn't really matter. It was just part of the creative process. The results are what matters.''

Her discomfort piqued his curiosity. He crossed his arms over his chest. "Yeah, well, since I've just been signed on to the Jill Hershey Modeling Agency, I'd like to know how it came about.''

She glanced away and waved her hand in a dismissing gesture. "It was just a silly remark. I'm sure you know Trina is a fan of yours.''

"What was the remark?"

She rearranged the location of a pencil holder on her desk. "Is this really necessary?"

"Yep."

She looked up and sighed. "She said you had the best backside of any doctor she'd ever seen."

"So you picked me for my butt. How shallow," he said in an amused voice. "I'm surprised at you."

"This is not about your butt," she said. "I chose you because you will photograph well and you embody the image of a true Texan and the possibility, the dream of a hero."

"It's about image and press."

She lifted her chin. "It's about understanding what the public's dreams are. I believe most people feel there has been a shortage of heroes. By using you, your image, and what you do we not only give people the dream of a hero, we offer them the opportunity to be heroes, too." She paused a half beat and could have knocked him flat with the expression in her gaze. "I dare you."

Silence followed, but Tyler felt as if a lightning bolt had cracked through him. Her passion, the same passion he felt, sparked from her eyes. Her cheeks were flushed with it. Her voice resonated with it. He felt an inexplicable promise of fulfillment, of a missing piece he hadn't thought was missing. In that moment he craved her in every way a man could crave a woman, and he'd never felt that way before.

He bit back an oath and tried to cover his confusion with a chuckle. "Okay, when do I strip?"

She blinked, and the color in her cheeks intensified. "You won't have to strip," she said weakly.

"Now I know why they call you a sorceress," he said.

"I'm not a sorceress," she quickly denied. "I just get the job done."

"No, you do more. You get people health care they need and give the contributors something they need. That's more than getting the job done." He held her gaze, the thread of connection drawing him while her eyes warned him off. "What about you, Jill? Who is your hero?"

The light in her eyes dimmed a little, but her posture remained erect. "I learned the hard way not to count on someone else to be my hero. I can be my own hero."

He felt a strange stinging sensation and fought the strangest, craziest desire to be her hero. Pushing the insanity inside, he replaced it with another. "What are you doing for dinner?"

"It's been a long day, but I'd like to sketch out some more ideas while they're fresh in my head. I'm eating at home," she said firmly.

I do not want to spend my evening with you, she might as well have said. Tyler got her message loud and clear. If he was the nice guy everyone thought he was, he would comply with her wishes; and if he told himself she wasn't worth his time, he would leave her alone.

Jill's doorbell rang at eight o'clock while she was listening to a classical music CD and writing potential ad slogans. Frowning, she glanced at the door and rose. Since she'd just arrived in Fort Worth a few days ago, she hadn't really made any friends, so she couldn't imagine who— She looked through the peephole and saw Tyler wearing a cocky grin and carrying a small brown paper bag.

She opened the door and blocked the doorway. She didn't want him in her temporary home tonight. The man took up entirely too much space of every room he entered. He could make a wheat field feel crowded.

"Hi," he said. "Since you fainted in my arms last night, I thought I should make sure you're okay tonight. No relapses?"

"Thank you. None. I'm fine."

"I forgot to tell you that TJ made it through the surgery today."

She felt a softening inside her. "Thank you. I'm glad to hear that. I'll have to go visit him."

He lifted the bag. "Also brought some Blue Bell ice cream to share with you and find out more about my modeling assignment."

Give up, Jill told herself. "Come in," she said, unable to conceal her reticence.

He gave a bad-boy grin and sauntered inside.

"You were going to let me stay out there all night." He made a tsking sound. "I can see you need some exposure to our Texan hospitality. What made you let me in? My smile, charm or great butt?"

Just for fun, she was sorely tempted to say his great butt. "Ice cream," she told him. "It's one of my five basic food groups."

He plastered a crestfallen expression on his face. "The ice cream was a bonus. I was supposed to be the main draw. I don't know if my ego can take this."

"Oh, I'm sure it can," she said. "Isn't it the biggest part of you?"

"Oh," he said, giving a rough chuckle and shaking his head. He moved closer, crowding her. "That's a terrible thing to say to a man. You know you're asking for trouble, don't you?"

Three

Uh-oh. Jill's heart slammed into her rib cage at the seductively predatory look on Tyler's face. She licked her lips. "I thought we decided you didn't need to flirt with me."

"You said that. Not me," he said, moving closer.

She took a step backward. Her heart still racing, she struggled to remain rational. "This is silly. You have an entire hospital full of women interested in you. The only reason you're doing this is because I'm not interested in you."

"You're not?" he said, his voice rippling over her nerve endings.

She took another step back. "I told you I'm here to do a job."

"And you're not at all attracted to me," he said.

Jill took another step and felt the wall behind her. "You're a flirt."

He nodded. "You don't like flirts."

"I haven't had good experience with flirts."

He went still for a moment and stared *into* her, not at her, into her, and she could almost swear he could read her. "Your husband was a flirt," he said, and gently lifted his hand to her cheek.

His touch made something inside her tumble free. She closed her eyes to fight the feeling.

"He was an idiot."

"How do you know?" she whispered, appalled at the burning sensation behind her eyes.

"He had you forever, but he let you go," he said, then his mouth touched hers.

His lips were warm and searching. She felt the same searching inside her. He brushed against her lips back and forth, coaxing, inviting. Jill opened, and he tasted her and she tasted him. She tugged gently on his bottom lip, and his groan vibrated in all her secret places. He pressed his chest against her and she immediately felt her nipples harden. His hand molded her jaw, caressing her. His tongue teased her, her brain clouded with his musky masculine scent, and she wanted more. She wanted his strong arms around her, his hard body pressed against hers. She wanted the rush and heat of passion. She wanted to make him lose his cocky control, and she wanted him to make her lose hers.

Her body straining toward his, she wanted. What she wanted was insanity.

Self-preservation trickled in and she turned her head and gasped for air. "This is crazy," she whispered. "Crazy, crazy, crazy, and not smart."

"Maybe," Tyler admitted. "But there's something between you and me that's—"

Jill groaned and covered her face with her hand. "You're not going to say this is bigger than the two of us, are you?"

He pulled her hand away. "No." His eyes grew serious. "But there's something between us I haven't felt before."

"Are you sure it isn't the way I say no?"

He tugged her hair. "I'm sure."

"Do you want me to tell you all the sensible reasons we shouldn't get involved?"

"No."

"But you're commitment shy or phobic, plus I'm not going to be here all that long," she told him.

"All the more reason not to waste time," he said. "To find out what it is."

"I don't think I'm cut out for this."

"What?" he asked, sliding his hand through her hair. "Not cut out for finding out how much you like me?"

"I didn't come here for this. I came here to get your wing and for me to—" She broke off, abruptly realizing she was disclosing more than she wanted.

His gaze intensified. "My wing and for you to what?"

She took a breath, brushed his hand away and stepped aside. "I have my reasons for accepting the job. Some are professional. Some are personal."

"What are they?"

The teeniest part of her wanted to unburden herself, but it would be a mistake to confide in Tyler. She needed to handle this on her own, and she didn't need a crazy whirlwind involvement with Dr. Cowboy. "I prefer not to discuss it."

"Maybe I can help."

"You can't," she said. "Let's just leave well enough alone."

He shook his head and gently smiled, his gaze promising that he wasn't done with her. That gaze put a mixture of dread and excitement in her heart and made her knees lose their starch. "Jill, honey," he said in a chiding voice, "you and I both know that well enough alone never is."

The woman bothered him. Tyler didn't know if it was the combination of pain and fire in her gaze or his itch to push past her prissy demeanor to find out what was underneath, but Jill Hershey bothered him. And now that he'd kissed her, she bothered him even more.

After he arrived at his apartment, he glanced at the starless night and tossed a tarp over his bike and walked inside. He didn't bother turning on the light. He was too restless for it.

Women didn't affect him this way. Yes, they aroused him. Yes, they amused him. But they didn't bother him. They didn't make him wonder if he might be missing something important. He frowned.

The phone rang, interrupting his dark mood. He answered it impatiently.

An extra second of silence followed. "Who spit in your cornflakes?"

Tyler chuckled at the sound of his older brother's voice. "Hi, Brock. What's up?"

"I just want to make sure you remember there's a wedding coming up and your presence is not optional."

Tyler grinned. "I wouldn't miss seeing you get yourself tied to Felicity for anything. She's not getting cold feet, is she?"

"Don't you worry about me or Felicity. I'm keeping her warm."

Tyler heard the sound of satisfaction in his brother's voice and felt a surprising tinge of envy. He shook his head at the feeling. "And you've decided the Logan Curse is a bunch of bull as I always said, right?"

"No, the Logan Curse is real. I just found the woman who can break it for me. You'll have to do the same for yourself."

Tyler snorted in disbelief.

"You go ahead and deny it sunup to sundown,"

Brock said. "But if you really didn't believe in the curse, you would have gotten serious with at least one woman by now."

"That's almost as much bull as the curse itself. I just haven't met a woman who made me want to get serious."

"I guess not, when you're doing the two-step so fast you probably can't see straight."

Tyler sighed. "Why is it that every time someone gets married they feel compelled to convert the rest of the world to matrimony?"

"Hell, I'm not trying to convert you. You can be Texas's most eligible bachelor for the rest of your life if you want."

With his recent photo assignment, Brock's comment stuck in his craw. Tyler stifled a growl.

"Met anyone new lately?"

"Not really," Tyler said, then relented. "Well sorta. PR consultant for the hospital. She wants to turn me into a poster-boy pinup to raise money for the new pediatric cardiology wing."

"Poster-boy pinup?" Brock echoed.

"Yep."

"Do you have to do it in the buff?"

"No," Tyler said, finding a sweet irony in the fact that his and his brother's minds worked the same way at times. "She seems to think my mug will bring in the dough," Tyler said in disgust.

"She must be impressed with you."

"Not enough to—" He broke off and swore under his breath.

"Not enough to what? Fall in bed at your first line like every other woman."

"Stuff it, Brock," Tyler said, his impatience soaring again. "You know I don't take every woman I meet or even date to bed. This woman, she—" he made a sound of exasperation "—she doesn't like flirts."

Brock barked in laughter, and Tyler pulled the receiver away from his ear to glare at it.

He brought it back into place and frowned. "You're not helping."

"Sorry," he said, continuing to chuckle. "It's just so satisfying to see you come up against a woman who doesn't fall for your charms right off the bat. Looks like you've got a challenge in front of you."

"I just need to get her out of my system," Tyler said, his restlessness grating on him like fingernails on a chalkboard.

"That's what I said about Felicity. And the wedding's in three and a half weeks," Brock reminded him with another chuckle. "Bring her down for the weekend. I'd like to meet her."

Jill's sound machine was set to ocean waves; the sun danced on a suncatcher in her office window; her door was closed. All was at peace.

A sharp rap followed that thought, and her door

burst open to reveal the man responsible for her lack of sleep last night.

"Hi," Tyler said, "I've been doing some thinking about this modeling business—"

Jill heard Trina squeal with delight. "They're beautiful!" Her assistant brought a bouquet of flowers and small package to her desk. "Look what just arrived for you. Who are they from?" Her attention quickly shifted to Tyler. "Oh, Dr. Logan. Jill gave me some questions I need to ask you to prepare the press for you."

Tyler's gaze was on the flowers. "Who sent them?"

"I don't know," she murmured, opening the card and wishing she didn't have an audience. It read: "Don't forget. Think about my offer. Love, Gordon."

"Oh," she said, unable to swallow her sigh. She had already thought about his offer and told him she wasn't ready for a long-term commitment with him even though she knew Gordon was what she'd said she wanted. He was kind, stable, not interested in having children, and he wasn't a flirt.

"Who sent them?" Tyler asked, walking over to the desk and touching a few of the roses in the arrangement.

Jill wished he would move away from her, she thought with a tinge of resentment as every inch of his six foot body emanated curiosity. She wished he would back off. Like maybe to Oklahoma. Maybe then her heart wouldn't jump and sputter. "My boss," she said, putting the arrangement on the other side of her desk so Tyler would keep his hands off it.

"I wish my boss would send me flowers like that," Trina said wistfully, then glanced at Tyler. "I wish anyone would send me flowers like that."

"He often sends flowers to us when we start a new out-of-town assignment," Jill said.

"What does the card say?" Tyler asked.

Jill blinked. "Why do you need to know?"

"Just curious."

"You still have a package to open," Trina said. "Let me get those questions, Dr. Logan."

Trina was back in a flash while Jill tore the paper.

"What is your favorite food?"

"I have two. Steak and ice cream. How did you like the Blue Bell ice cream I brought you last night?" he asked Jill.

Feeling Trina's curious gaze, she cleared her throat. "It was delicious. Thank you."

"Did you save any for me?"

She shook her head, feeling sheepish. She had felt incredibly deprived after Tyler had left, so it had been easy for her to polish off the double portion of ice cream.

"You ate all of it?" he asked incredulously.

She smiled. "When it comes to ice cream, it's every man for himself, or woman for herself."

"Your favorite extracurricular activities?" Trina interjected.

"Visiting my family ranch," Tyler said. "I don't have much time for that, let alone anything else. And I like to two-step with the right woman."

"I like to two-step, too," Trina said.

Jill rolled her eyes. "I can't."

"What's your favorite color?"

Jill felt his gaze on her from head to toe.

"Navy-blue," he said with the devil in his eyes.

She was wearing navy-blue. Her heart skipped a beat, and she turned her attention to the package and opened it.

"Your favorite music?"

"Country, of course," Tyler said.

Jill stared down at the framed photo of her boss and felt her stomach sink. "Don't forget me," a small slip of his notepaper said. When Trina and Tyler craned to see it, she quickly folded the note in her palm.

Tyler lifted an eyebrow. "Who is that?"

"Uh, my boss," Jill said, wishing she could make Tyler and her assistant disappear.

"Really?" Trina studied the photo. "He looks a little stiff."

"Think so?" Tyler said with a slight snicker. "Looks like a fun guy to me."

Gordon's face was so solemn he almost looked funereal. Jill put the photo on the opposite corner of her desk and defended him. "Gordon is a gentleman, very stable, and he isn't a flirt."

"Sounds like an old gelding my brother has at the ranch," Tyler said.

Trina giggled.

Jill gave her a withering glance and resisted the urge to stomp her foot and scream. In the space of five minutes, her peaceful office had turned into a three-ring circus.

Trina's phone rang, relieving her of one of the rings.

Jill turned back to Tyler. "You had a question about your modeling assignment?"

"Yeah, but I'd also like to know more about Gordie, here," he said.

She tapped her foot, the sound of her impatience muffled by the carpet. "I've already told you about him, and you've seen his picture and his taste in flowers."

"And his taste in women," he concluded, looking at her curiously. "Does he turn you on?"

"That's really none of your business, but turning each other on may not always be the most important thing in a relationship. There are respect, kindness, loyalty—"

"You can get those from your horse."

Jill counted to ten. "I don't have a horse." She redirected the conversation once more. "You had a question about the modeling?"

Tyler put his hands on his hips and sighed. "Yeah. What kind of compensation do I get?"

Jill did a double take. "All of the money earned as a result of your pictures will be donated to the new wing. Isn't that what you wanted?"

"That's okay," Tyler said. "But it occured to me that a lot of people, including hospital employees, will benefit from the wing, but since I'm the one working the gig, there should be something extra in it for me. Don't you agree?"

Her jaw worked in silence. It was difficult for her to disagree, but— She shrugged. "What did you have in mind?"

"Since I'm doing something for you, I'd like you to do some things for me," he said with a glint in his eye that made the hair on the back of her neck stand up.

Wary, she tried to read him. "What 'things'?"

He chuckled. "Don't worry. It doesn't involve pictures or billboards. You can keep your clothes on," he said, then added, "if you want."

Her stomach dipped at the lazy invitation in his eyes. "What 'things'?" she repeated.

"Just a few field trips. A trip to a ranch, visiting a few famous Fort Worth landmarks. We'll start with the ranch this weekend," he said.

Jill's heart flew into her throat. She coughed. She wanted to decrease her proximity to Tyler, not increase it. "W-w-wait a minute. This weekend? As in forty-eight hours?"

He nodded. "Yep."

"That's too soon."

"When will the photographer start snapping at me?"

"He won't snap," she said. "At least not that way. He starts today. He'll follow you around."

"Would you like that? Having a photographer follow you around, watching your every move?"

"No, but your ego is bigger than—"

He pressed his finger over her lips, his laser-blue eyes inches from hers. "We're not going to start talking about size again, are we?" He traced the shape of her mouth with his finger.

Jill's mouth went dry.

"If the photographer's going to dog me today, then you can take a little trip to West Texas this weekend."

"I...I really don't think this is necessary."

"Maybe, but it's fair," he said. "If I'm putting my mug on billboards and losing my privacy for the sake of the wing, then you should be willing to take a few field trips, don't you think?"

She didn't agree with his reasoning, but she couldn't exactly argue with it, either. "But why?"

"I get my curiosity satisfied," he said, his glance heating her from head to toe, "if nothing else. And my curiosity is a powerful thing. Bigger than my ego," he said with an edge to his voice. "I bet yours is, too. Pack your jeans. We'll take my bike," he told her, and his lips twitched. "Maybe you can try

out that gelding while I'm there and see if you like
the ride he gives you.''

Jill spent the rest of the afternoon supervising the
shoot of Tyler's pictures and trying to think of a
way to get out of going on the weekend outing.
Tyler indulged the photographer for nearly three
hours, then told the man to get lost.

By the end of the day she was exhausted, but she
had one more thing to do. Jill hadn't forgotten her
original purpose for coming to Fort Worth General
Hospital. Yes, she intended to make the project for
the wing a bang-up success, but she also intended
to conquer her past. It was time to take another step.

With ammonia salts in her suit jacket pocket, she
walked to the elevator and pushed the floor for the
nursery. Watching the numbers illuminate as she
passed each floor, she took a deep breath when the
elevator stopped and the doors whooshed open.

''I can do this,'' she whispered, and slowly
walked down the hall.

''I can do this,'' she whispered again clenching
her fists and biting her lip. Her hands grew clammy
as the sight of the nursery windows came into view.
She slowed even more and took deep, even breaths.

She stepped in front of the large windows and
closed her eyes to steady herself. Then she carefully
opened them and looked at the array of layettes
filled with infants wrapped like mummies in blue

and pink blankets. Most were sleeping. A few cried, their tiny faces straining with exertion.

She touched her tummy, remembering, wishing she had been able to see her precious baby screaming his lungs out in the hospital nursery. She wished she had a memory, just one, of holding her grasshopper alive in her arms. The emptiness twisted her heart and she felt tears stream down her cheeks.

From the glare of the lights, Jill saw her reflection in the nursery window and shoved her hands in her pockets in search of a tissue. "Damn," she muttered under her breath, swiping at her tears. Ammonia didn't do a thing for a runny nose.

A handkerchief was pressed into her hand, and she glanced into the reflection of the window again. Her heart raced. Tyler, towering over her, gazing down at her.

He'd caught her. Worse yet, he'd caught her crying. Maybe fainting wouldn't be such a bad idea right now, after all.

She felt his arms close around her and was too surprised to speak. She stiffly allowed him to hold her, overwhelmed at the warmth and comfort he generated.

"I know one of your secrets now," he said.

She tensed, closing her eyes. She didn't want him knowing secrets about her.

"Babies make you cry."

He said it so simply, as if she were like a million others who got a little weepy at the sight of newborns. She smiled at the same time her stomach clenched. He'd given her an out. She could like him for that. His flirting wouldn't get her, but his kindness could. He was dangerous, but she'd sensed that from the beginning.

"You're right," she said, looking into laser-blue eyes that saw too much. "Babies make me cry." If she had her way, he'd never learn why.

Four

Opening her door to Tyler on Friday afternoon, she gave it one last try. Jill had a very strong feeling this field trip was *not* a good idea. "I'm not really a ranch person."

He shifted his helmet to his hip and pulled his sunglasses off his face. "That's okay. I'm not cut out for modeling, either. I'll get your bag," he said, and brushed past her.

"That's not necessary," Jill said, rushing after him as he took the steps two at a time. She couldn't help noticing his long, strong legs and very nice— She cut off the thought. "I've got a few more things to put in my suitcase."

He rounded the corner to her bedroom. "Can't

take a suitcase on the motorcycle. If you don't have a duffel bag, I have room in mine."

"But—"

She watched him scoop up her lingerie, jeans and shirts in one fell swoop. "Got a bag?" he asked her.

Something about the sight of his fingers wrapped around her panties and bras gave her the hiccups. Spurred into action, she grabbed a tote bag from the closet and reached for her clothes. "This should work," she said, blindly forcing the clothes into the bag.

She glanced up to find him holding a lone pair of purple French-cut silk panties. He looked at the panties, then his gaze drifted over her breasts and lower to her hips. She felt his gaze like a touch. His eyes met hers, and his expression brought a scaldingly sexual visual to her mind.

Sex.

Jill couldn't remember the last time she'd been in the mood for sex. It had been at least three years.

Fighting the heat rising from her toes to her cheeks, she snatched the scrap of silk from his hands and crammed it into the bag. "Let me grab a few toiletries."

In the master bath, she threw a few basics into a smaller bag. Her mind screaming a dozen protests, she returned to the bedroom. There he stood, next to her bed, dressed in leather and denim, taking up too much space and too much oxygen, namely hers.

Heaven help her, how was she going to get through this weekend?

"I'm ready," she muttered, and shoved the toiletry bag into the tote.

His lips twitched. "Think of it as a broadening experience."

"The only reason I'm going is because I've seen the first batch of your photos."

He grinned. "I must be too good to resist."

"You're right," she said, stomping down the stairs. "The public won't be able to resist you." But she would. She had to. He led the way outside, and Jill locked the door behind her. "How far away is the ranch?"

"About a hundred and sixty miles," he said. "We can use the microphones so you don't get bored."

"Microphones?"

"Microphones so we can talk while we're riding on my bike," he said, putting her bag in a compartment in the back of the motorcycle.

She looked at Tyler's big black bike, and that was when it hit her. In the back of her mind she had known she would be joining him on the bike, but she must have pushed the fact that her body would be pressed intimately against his for over two hours from her mind. She quickly calculated miles and time and bit her lip.

Two and a half hours of being wrapped around Dr. Tyler Logan. Trina would be in ecstasy. Jill would be in hell. She was beginning to think that Tyler was to her what kryptonite was to a certain superhero. Disaster.

During the first thirty miles, Jill played mind games with herself. Tyler was everything she didn't want in a man, she told herself as her fingers curled into his taut abdomen through his T-shirt. She didn't like the way his back felt against her breasts. She didn't like the way he smelled, a seductive mix of musk and masculinity. She didn't like the way his dark hair curled slightly at his nape. For that matter, she didn't like the way the man breathed.

"Tell me about Gordie."

She heard his voice through her earphone and blinked. "Gordie?"

"Yeah, the guy who sent the flowers and the bad picture."

"The picture wasn't bad," she said, defending Gordon.

"It wasn't?" He chuckled. "Poor guy."

"That wasn't nice. Gordon is a kind man. He's very stable, very even-tempered, very—"

"Boring."

"That's not fair."

"But true. What do you like about him? That he's not threatening? That he doesn't ruffle your feathers?"

"I appreciate his intelligence and stability. He's very loyal."

"I told you he sounds like a gelding at the ranch."

Jill just groaned.

"Looks like he wants to be more than your boss," Tyler said. "How do you feel about that?"

Jill shifted uncomfortably. "Gordon has many wonderful qualities. Any woman would be fortunate to be involved with him."

"Which means you're not interested."

"I didn't say that."

"Yeah, but you weren't enthusiastic. You still could have been talking about the gelding or a faithful dog. No passion."

The wind whipping at her face and hair, Jill glared at his back. "Passion is overrated."

"If you had experienced true passion you wouldn't say that."

"I suppose you have."

"I've gotten close. But I've seen the real thing in action between my brother and his fiancée. You'll see what I mean when you meet them. They're getting married in a few weeks."

"Does she have a ranching background?" Jill asked, thinking that would be necessary for marriage to a rancher.

Tyler chuckled. "None, zero, zip. Felicity lived in Manhattan her entire life, but now she has seen the light and she realizes Texas is the best place anyone could live."

Jill's lips twitched at his state pride. "Have you ever been to Hawaii?"

"Nice place to visit, but Texas is the best place to live. Keep your eyes open and you might see the light, too."

Jill kept her eyes open for the rest of the ride despite the monotonous landscape. By the time Tyler pulled into the long driveway, she was more than ready to dismount the bike.

Her knees buckled when she slid over the side, and Tyler caught her. "Whoa. Take your time."

"My knees feel like jelly and my bottom is numb."

"Need a massage?" he offered with a bad-boy grin, and skimmed his hand over her hip.

Her heart jolted and she stumbled backward. "No. I'll be fine in a minute."

"Uncle Tyler!" a young girl and boy chorused from the porch, then ran toward him.

"Hey, you guys, come here and meet someone," Tyler shouted, then said to Jill, "My two favorite angels or brats…depending on the day."

He swung both up in his arms and the sight of the two kids smiling and laughing tugged at Jill's heart. "Dad had to check on a herd near the stream, but Felicity got Addie to bake *two* chocolate pies!" the girl said.

"Felicity is the best thing that's happened to this place since—" Tyler broke off, looking at the kids and grinning. "—since *you!* How's school going?"

"I made the honor roll," the girl said.

"You always make the honor roll," the boy said, then grinned with pride. "I did, too."

"Way to go. We have geniuses," Tyler said, giving each a high-five. He turned them to face Jill. "Jill Hershey, I'd like you to meet the two smartest, best kids in Texas—my nephew Jacob and my niece, Bree. Jill is a public relations sorceress who is going to get my hospital a new wing for pediatric cardiology patients."

"A sorceress?" Bree echoed, her Logan eyes bright with curiosity.

"It's nice to meet you both. Your uncle is exaggerating. Has he ever done that before?"

Bree waved her hand. "Oh, all the time. You must be pretty good if he called you a sorceress, though. Uncle Tyler doesn't believe in magic or curses."

"Well, I do!" The cultured yet warm voice drew everyone's attention.

Jill looked at the slim, smiling, attractive woman and felt like a hillbilly cousin.

Tyler grinned. "Flip, you're looking more like a rancher's wife every day," he said, taking in her silk blouse and slacks.

"There you go criticizing my clothes again. I wanted to look nice for your visitor," she said, and added meaningfully, "a *woman*." She extended her hand to Jill. "Welcome. I'm Felicity. Would you like something to drink and a chance to freshen up?''

"Thank you. That would be nice.''

"Brock should be back soon,'' Felicity said.

"The Coltranes again?'' Tyler asked with a grimace.

"Of course. I asked him if he wanted me to beat them up, but—'' She broke off with a shrug.

"Let me guess. After he stopped laughing he said no.''

Felicity's lips twitched. "How'd you guess? Come on, Jill. Let me show you around.''

She followed Felicity's lead while the kids bounced along beside them. "Felicity, will you play piano with me today?'' Jacob asked.

"I was going to ask her,'' Bree said.

"Why don't you play with me?'' Tyler asked, and Jill nearly tripped in surprise.

"*You* play the piano?''

"I'm a man of many talents,'' he told her with the barest invitation in his voice. "You should take the time to find out about all of them.''

"I'm sure there are too many for me to fathom in the short time I'll be in Texas,'' she said sweetly.

"Touché,'' Felicity said, and hooked her arm through Jill's. "I like her. Can I borrow her from Fort Worth on a regular basis?''

"I don't know how Brock will feel about having two city girls around.''

"He'll love it," Felicity said with a confident smile. "He likes city girls now."

Felicity led the way up the wooden porch of the large home. When she walked through the door, Jill immediately felt a sense of history. Spotting the portraits of family members on the wall and smelling the scent of polished wood, she soaked in the atmosphere. "Wow," she said, "I can feel the generations."

Felicity nodded. "It was the same for me the first time I came here, too. It sounds strange, but there's a lot of emotion in these walls. Here's the kitchen and dining room. Let me get you some lemonade," Felicity said and poured a glass from a pitcher in the refrigerator. "Down the hall is the library which I invaded when I arrived."

Jill peeked in the large room featuring a desk and a baby grand piano. The windows were bare except for a blue satin header at the top. Feeling an odd bittersweet tug, she walked in and spotted the portrait of a lovely woman on the wall. "Who is she?"

"Brock, Tyler and Martina's mother. She's lovely, isn't she?"

"Yes." There was a lively gentleness in the woman's eyes. She had seen it echoed in Tyler. The thought softened her heart.

"The men adored her. She taught both boys to play piano. Martina didn't get a chance. Her mother died giving birth to her."

Jill's chest tightened, her own experience haunting her. "Tyler told me. How terrible."

"Yes, it was. Their father shut himself off after that, and I think all the children suffered, perhaps Tyler and Martina the most."

"Why Tyler and Martina?"

"Brock was always going to do the ranch, so he got some attention from that. But Tyler," Felicity said with a grin, "was destined for something different. Brock stood up for him, but Tyler's had a tough road. And Martina looked so much like her mother that Papa Logan couldn't bear to look at her. It's a miracle they turned out so well."

Her respect for Tyler grew. He could have become a much different person, bitter, fearful. Instead, he fixed children's broken hearts.

"And then there's the curse," Felicity said with a groan.

"The curse," Jill echoed, then remembered Tyler mentioning it before. "I think Tyler told me something about it. He said he didn't believe in it."

Felicity gave a snort. "The advantage with Brock was that he did believe in it. That meant all I had to do was break it."

"And how did you do that?" she asked, because she didn't put much stock in magic or curses.

Felicity smiled. "Lots of candles, lots of love, and a lot of risk. The trouble with Tyler is that he *says* he doesn't believe the curse, but he acts as though he believes it."

"Why do you say that?"

"He won't get serious with a woman."

"Maybe he hasn't met the right woman yet."

Felicity gave her an assessing glace. "I can hope, can't I? It will take a special woman to love Tyler the way he needs to be loved. She'll need to be strong in her own right, be able to see past his flirting."

"He's a terrible flirt," Jill said.

"Yes, he is, but he's very perceptive, and I can't think of a man with a bigger heart," she said. "Except Brock."

Jill wondered what it must be like to love a man as much as Felicity clearly loved Brock. It seemed a scary yet brave prospect. She thought she had loved her husband, but not with the power Felicity emanated. Glancing back at the picture of Tyler's mother, she looked at the lively, gentle eyes and felt something inside her shift. She felt a kinship with the woman who had lost her life while giving life. Jill would have done the same for her baby, but hadn't been given the option.

Jill wondered what Tyler had been like as a child, how he had dealt with such a great loss and the lack of approval and support from his father. She wondered what was behind the flirt.

Tyler felt Jill's gaze on him throughout the dinner meal. He was accustomed to female attention. He flirted with women, and women flirted back. At times they initiated; at times they seduced.

Most, however, didn't gaze at him as if they wanted to see beneath his skin, into his brain, maybe into his heart. Tyler had always been led to believe he had enough going for him on the outside that they didn't bother to take the trouble to look inside. That was fine because seeing deeper would have brought more trouble than he wanted.

Normally Jill's intense attention would have worked for him in a big way. There was a slight edge of sensuality in her gaze, but mostly there was curiosity. Deeper curiosity. Uh-oh, he thought, then grinned to himself. Maybe he could distract her. Distraction had always worked before.

"Let me show you our horses," Tyler said. "You probably need a break from the indoor barnyard."

"Indoor barnyard?" Tyler's older brother, Brock, said with a lifted eyebrow. "Were you speaking of your usual bull?"

Tyler gave a long-suffering sigh and walked to Jill's side. "You can't get off the subject of cattle."

"Sure I can. Especially when the woman in my life insists on serving chicken for dinner."

Felicity put her hand over Brock's and gave a softly amused smile. "You didn't enjoy your meal, sweetheart?"

"No. I enjoyed it, but I'm president of the local chapter of the Cattlemen's Association."

"Your secret is safe with us," Felicity said.

"Let's get while the getting's good," Tyler whispered to Jill. "The great vegetarian debate will begin any minute."

Jill stood. "Thank you for dinner. It was delicious," she murmured.

"Anytime, Jill," Brock said. "And maybe next time we'll have calf fries for you."

Felicity grimaced. "With vegetarian chili."

Tyler tugged Jill out the door. "Told you so."

"Who will win the argument?"

"Neither or both." He pushed open the screen door and led her down the steps. "Depends on your point of view. Nice night."

"What does that mean?"

"They'll settle the argument by making love."

Jill paused, then chuckled. "Oh. And calf fries?"

"Fried calf testicles," he told her, guiding her down the driveway toward the barn.

She gaped at him. "You don't really eat them."

"They're considered a delicacy."

"By the Cattlemen's Association," she said, rolling her eyes.

"Probably," he said. "I'd be just as happy with a pizza, but don't tell my brother."

"Ah," she said with a mysterious smile, "one of your secrets."

He slid his hand underneath the hair of her nape. "I didn't notice this dress mixed in with your jeans and girlie things."

"You seemed to be more interested in the girlie things," Jill said wryly.

He looked into her eyes and felt an odd tug inside him. "I like the way your eyes shine in the moonlight."

Her lids slid downward, hiding her eyes from him. "Tyler," she said in a husky, sexy voice that felt like a stroke over key erogenous zones.

He dipped his head.

She glanced up, her gaze direct and honest. "It's a beautiful evening. Don't ruin it by giving me a bunch of lines."

He gave a self-deprecating chuckle and shook his head. "You're a hard woman, Jill. C'mon and meet my ponies."

He led her into the cool barn and introduced the horses one by one. Ladies first, then the boys. He noticed the way she mimicked his touch on the horses. "This is the gelding I told you about. Eddie boy here is as gentle and loyal as a dog."

Jill stroked his coat and met his gaze. "I've heard riding a gelding is preferable to riding a stallion."

"Depends on the kind of ride you want," he said. "Most people probably prefer a gelding. If you were dressed differently we could find out. Not that I mind your dress. You've got great legs."

"No lines," she began, lifting her finger.

He closed his hand around her slim finger and met her doubtful gaze. "No line. Deal with it, Jill. You've got great legs."

Glancing down, he noticed her sandal strap was twisted. He knelt down and untwisted it.

"What are you—"

He wrapped his hand around her ankle and rubbed his thumb over her smooth skin. "You have small ankles. Do you work out?"

He watched her swallow. "I run sometimes."

"It shows," he said, skimming his hand up her calf, behind her knee to the inside of her thigh. She stopped his wandering hand.

He met her gaze. "Does it bother you for me to touch you?"

"It's distracting," she said, her gaze smoky. "But you know that. I know you're a flirt, you've succeeded in arousing—" her lips lifting in a feminine smile that tugged at his loins, she urged him to stand and rested her hand on his chest "—my curiosity. I want to know what's behind the flirt."

Five

Her directness aroused him at the same time his gut tightened into a knot. "What makes you think I'm more than a flirt?"

"Woman's intuition," she said. "So tell me what made you go into medicine."

"I guess this means you won't go for the 'babes love it' response."

She shook her head and shot him a chiding glance. "I want the truth, the real reason."

Tyler had an itchy feeling about this woman. At the moment he wasn't sure if that was good or bad. He only knew he liked the way her hand felt on his chest and the way her eyes were fastened on him as if he were the only man in the world.

"I wanted to make a difference," he said. "I loved growing up on a ranch, but I always knew I would need to do something different. I clicked with medicine, and my specialty was something that makes a huge improvement in the quality of life of my patients. It's like taking somebody from darkness to light. I can't imagine anything more rewarding. I think my mother sensed I wouldn't be a rancher even when I was young, but my dad never accepted it."

"He never wanted to say, 'my son the doctor.'"

Tyler shook his head and grinned. "He would have preferred a large-animal veterinarian."

"How did you get past his lack of approval?"

He gave a wry chuckle, but felt his smile fade. "I never have. I keep waiting for him to come back and say 'You did good, son.'"

She started to remove her palm from his chest, but he covered her hand with his. "I want to make love to you."

Jill's eyes widened, and he watched her throat work to swallow.

"Not flirting," he said before she could protest. He skimmed his finger up her throat. "I'm stating a desire." He hesitated briefly, mentally rebelling at his second thought, then shrugged off the debate. "Maybe more than a desire. Maybe a need," he said, and watched her eyes grow even wider. He grinned despite his arousal. "You're not surprised."

"*Need* is a strong word."

He nodded, skimming his finger down her throat to her collarbone. "*Want* isn't strong enough."

She swallowed again, and he felt himself sweat with the need to take her lips. "Why me?" she asked.

"Because I have this gut feeling about you that you are either going to be very good for me. Or very bad." He lowered his head. "Either way, I want to find out."

He pressed his mouth against hers and gently tugged at her lower lip. Catching her nearly inaudible moan, he deepened the kiss and pulled her against him. It felt to him as if her body had been designed to mesh with his. Her breasts rubbed against his chest, her abdomen slid against his. Lower still, he wanted to rock between her creamy thighs. She wore a dress, but no stockings, just a pair of those silk, French-cut panties he held in his hand earlier.

He skimmed his hand down to her bottom and drew her dress upward until his fingers encountered her bare flesh. He squeezed her bottom and ground her against the part of him that swelled with need for her.

Clinging to his shirt, she strained against him, wrapping her tongue around his and gently sucking, echoing the movements of his pelvis. Then, making a sound of frustrated desire, she turned her head away from his and gasped for air.

"I'm not sure this is a good idea." She stepped away from him.

Tyler asked the first thing that came to mind. "Do you not like sex?"

She stared at him in shock. "I like sex," she finally managed. "I just haven't been in the mood for a while."

"How long a while?"

Jill winced self-consciously. "Do we really need to discuss this?"

"I'd say so. A few more minutes and I would have been inside you, and don't deny you weren't wanting it, too."

She covered her eyes with her hand. "I'm not denying it," she confessed in a low voice.

"Then how long have you not been in a mood?"

She shot him a look of irritation. "Since my marriage was over."

Now it was his turn to be surprised. "That long? Hell, was he that good in bed?"

Jill sighed. "No. It was just the way it ended. He left three months after I got out of the hospital. I hadn't fully recovered from the accident and—"

Tyler lifted his hands. "Whoa! Hospital? What accident?"

"I was in an automobile accident. A truck hit me head-on. I broke some bones, lost some blood and—" She broke off, flinching.

"And?" he prompted.

Not meeting his gaze, she took a slow breath. "I

broke some bones, lost some blood and lost my baby.''

Tyler felt as if he'd been punched. "Baby," he said, not knowing what to say. "How far along?"

"Seven months," she said in a voice devoid of hope.

"Viable. They couldn't save—"

"Him," she said. "They couldn't save him. He lost too much blood. His lungs were filled with fluid. It was a terrible accident. They said I could have died, too."

And, Tyler heard by the pain in her voice, there had been moments she'd wished she had died. He felt his chest tighten. He couldn't not hold her. As he pulled her into his arms, he said, "That's why babies make you cry."

She nodded against his shoulder.

"How could your husband leave you?" he demanded in disgust.

"He couldn't handle it. Some people can't." She paused. "I almost couldn't."

His mind racing, he held her tightly. "This is part of the reason you came to Fort Worth, isn't it?"

"Yes, to face my waterloo and move on." She looked up at him and gave a small but brave smile. "You dared me."

His heart turned over. He'd had no idea what he'd been asking of her. Now he was struck with the overwhelming urge to fix it, to heal her. Now. "I dare you to make love with me."

Her eyes widened, then she closed them and shook her head, chuckling. "I don't believe you. I tell you I lost a baby and you want to have sex?"

"You underestimate the power of making love," he corrected her, wanting to hold her and make her pain go away. "It's healing, life giving. I can do that for you."

She gave him a sideways glance, but her smile made him feel as if he'd just invented a new surgical procedure.

"A heart doctor," she said. "You're not talking about touching my heart. You're talking about touching—" her color rose "—other places."

He lifted his hand to her cheek. "I'm talking about touching everything, Jill. Everything."

Sparks of passion and wariness glinted in her eyes. "No," she finally said softly.

"You don't want me?"

Her breath hitched in her throat. "I didn't say that," she said.

Realization hit him. "Then you're chicken," he murmured, surprised.

She pulled away from him. "I'm not chicken. No one has ever called me chicken. Just because I have the good sense not to hit the sack with Dr. Romeo does not make me a chicken."

"Cluck, cluck," he said. "And you know that Romeo reputation stuff is a bunch of bull. Besides," he said, goading her, "we don't have to hit the sack. There are other ways."

Her cheeks lit with color again. "You were much easier to deal with when I thought you were a superficial flirt."

"You never thought I was just a superficial flirt, or you wouldn't have taken my dare. You always knew there was more to me," he said, then added under his breath, "as much as I conceal it. I think you knew I was going to be important to you, the same way I think you're going to be important to me."

"What about the curse?"

Tyler's eye twitched. "What curse?"

"The Logan Curse."

"I don't believe in it," he said. "It doesn't apply to us because neither of us wants to get married."

"Why don't you?" she asked, her curious eyes making him uncomfortable.

"It's not necessary," he said.

"Not necessary?"

"Not necessary to tie yourself down, put your heart, soul and future into a woman. It's too much to ask of a woman. Even if they want to stick with you," he said, thinking of his mother, "sometimes they can't."

Silence stretched between them. Tyler didn't like the knowing expression on her face. "What?" he demanded, his eye twitching again. "What?"

"Two words come to mind," she said with a gentle commiserating smile. "Cluck, cluck."

* * *

"I do not believe in that stupid curse," Tyler insisted to Brock as they stood in the parlor. His eyelid began to twitch.

"Sure you don't," Brock said with the same tone of complete and utter disbelief. "That's why you never let a woman get too close. You never let them get under your skin. Except I think Jill could be different."

"Jill is different," he conceded. "But she won't get under my skin. I'm not interested in forever, and neither is she."

"Why not? Why wouldn't you want forever with the right woman?"

"Because forever rarely is forever. Forever doesn't even usually last a lifetime." Tyler shook his head. "Ever since you and Felicity finally worked it out, you've been hounding me. You must have forgotten how you almost messed everything up."

Brock's expression grew serious. "I haven't forgotten. I just don't want you to mess up the same way I did."

Tyler paused, letting his brother's statement sink in. Brock had stood up for Tyler with their father, and although Brock wasn't a father figure, Tyler loved him and respected him so much it had nearly killed Tyler when he'd had to leave the ranch to practice in Fort Worth. He hadn't wanted to disappoint him. Brock had balked, but only for a moment. Since then, he'd been all support.

Tyler hitched his thumbs in his belt loops and sighed. "Okay. What's your point?"

Brock put his hand on Tyler's shoulder. "I married the wrong woman, then found the right one, but the curse almost cost me Felicity. The curse isn't that we lose the woman. We lose the ability to see her."

Tyler grunted. That was pretty deep for Brock. This once he wouldn't verbally disagree, since he could see Brock was sincere, but he wasn't sure he bought it.

The front door flew open and Martina breezed in with a smile on her face. "Hi, boys. Surprise. I talked to Felicity yesterday and she told me Tyler was here with a *woman,* so I had to come see."

His sister, who was the spitting image of their mother, wore a loose-fitting top that almost concealed her early pregnancy.

She looked from one to the other. "Oops. You both look serious. You're either discussing cattle futures or the ongoing feud with the Coltranes?" Her voice rose the slightest bit when she mentioned the Coltranes.

"Neither," Brock said. "Although they've started another harebrained scheme for their ranch."

"Noah's going to run a fencing camp during the winter and charge a fortune. Crazy," he muttered.

"I believe it's referred to as ranch management," she said with a cheeky grin. "Have you heard anything else about him?"

"Not much since he got back from Chicago. Come to think of it, he came back soon after you did." He chuckled. "Think about it. You could have run into Noah Coltrane in Chicago, when we've successfully avoided most dealings with them all our lives."

Her smile wavered. "That would have been something, wouldn't it?" She lifted her chin. "Don't try to distract me. What dire topic were you discussing when I walked in?"

"The Logan Curse," Brock said.

"Oh," she said, waving her hand in a dismissing gesture. "I've got that covered. Have you noticed the Logan women are the ones who croak? Well," she said with a triumphant smile, "I'm never getting married. That way I cheat the curse."

Brock groaned and rubbed his face. He walked toward her and led her to the couch. "Sit down and act like a pregnant woman should. Have you been eating right?"

"Have you kept regular appointments with your doctor?"

"Yes and yes."

"Who is the father?" Brock and Tyler asked at once.

She gave them each a pained glance. "I told you the stork did it."

"We heard a lot of noise. What's going on?" Felicity asked, bringing Jill with her into the room. Felicity's face lit up. "Martina, you came!"

Tugging Jill alongside her, Felicity rushed to Martina and the two women embraced. "Jill Hershey, this is Martina."

Martina gave Jill an assessing glance. "I understand you're going to plaster my brother all over billboards in Fort Worth for the sake of charity. Are you sure his head will fit?"

Jill's lips twitched and she met Tyler's gaze. "Gosh, your own sister seems to think your ego is the biggest—"

"My sister hasn't seen everything," Tyler said.

"Oooh," Martina said, and made a hissing, sizzling sound. "I like this one, but I'm still not sure how they'll fit your entire head on a billboard."

"We have an excellent photographer," Jill said, and softened just a bit. "But the subject is pretty fascinating, too."

"That's her way of saying she picked me because I have a nice butt."

Felicity turned to her. "Are you going to kill him?"

"Of course. I'm just not sure which way to do it."

Martina's eyes grew wide and she touched her abdomen.

"What's wrong?" Brock asked.

She waved her hand. "Nothing. I think it's the baby moving. Little flutters. I'm not sure you can feel it yet." She drew his hand to her abdomen. "Can you?"

"Are you sure it isn't indigestion?" Brock asked.

"Let me try," Felicity said, kneeling beside her sister-in-law.

Tyler glanced at Jill and saw her bite her lip. She looked pale and stiff. He moved to her side and put his arm around her. "Okay?" he asked in her ear.

"Do you want to feel it?" Martina asked Jill.

Tyler heard Jill take in a sharp breath and tried to cover for her. "Not everyone needs to feel the results of the tortilla chips you ate on the drive from Dallas."

"No," Jill said. "That's okay. I'd love to feel your baby move." She gingerly moved forward and allowed Martina to guide her hand. She concentrated for a long moment, then smiled. "I can feel it. This one will keep you up nights once he or she gets a little bigger."

Martina nodded. "If I keep eating the way I have been, I'm going to outweigh my brothers. And I wasn't eating tortilla chips," she said to Tyler. "Plain corn-chips."

"Close enough," he said, and tugged Jill outside. He looked down at her. "Are you sure you're okay?"

Still pale, she took a deep breath and nodded. "Yes. That's actually a little step forward for me. I haven't felt someone else's baby move since the accident, and I didn't faint or fall apart." She gave a brave smile. "I was fine."

She was such a strong woman that her vulnerability tore at him. He slid his hand behind her nape and nudged her upward to kiss her. "You were better than fine."

The depth of her ordeal was beginning to sink in for Tyler. The physical trauma she must have experienced, the grief and then the abandonment by her husband. His mouth tightened. She had been brave to accept his dare. She had known there would be pain for her, but she'd done it, anyway. Tyler didn't think he'd ever admired a woman more. More alarming, he'd never wanted to possess a woman more, either.

Jill still needed her wave machine on Monday. Although she felt she had made tremendous progress in working past some of her pain, another issue had bubbled to the surface. And it was all Tyler's fault.

Sex.

Her hormones had been in the deep freeze for such a long time she'd gotten used to it. Now, she thought with a frown as she flipped through her CDs in search of something soothing and nonsensual, her hormones were thawing.

She scowled. She supposed she could just go to bed with him, but Jill had never figured out how to give her body and keep her heart. She wondered if there was a how-to book on the subject.

Her door burst open, and Trina brought in a fresh

bouquet of flowers. She lifted a brow. "Whoever it is he's consistent."

Jill sighed. Nobody in this hospital knocked. She grabbed the card and read it. She grimaced.

"Your boss?"

Jill nodded. "I guess I didn't make myself as clear as I should have."

Trina shook her head. "Sometimes you have to hit 'em over the head with a frying pan."

"Hit who?" Tyler asked, striding into the room. "Morning, beautiful," he said to Jill.

Trina blushed and took the greeting for herself. "Thank you. Did you see Jill's new flowers?"

His grin faltered. "How about that. Persistent booger, isn't he?" He eyed the flowers. "What are you going to do with them?"

"She's going to keep them," Trina said. "They're beautiful."

Curious, Jill watched him. "What did you have in mind?"

He began to pace in that slide strut that drew attention to his long legs and height. "Sometimes when people get flowers they don't want," he said, and quickly amended, "or can't use, they give them to a patient. An elderly lady recovering from surgery or a teenager stuck in traction." He shrugged. "Just a thought," he said. "If you don't want—" he grinned "—or can't use them."

"I'll think about that. In the meantime, today is

another photo day for you.'' She glanced at his hair, face and eyes. ''Are you ready?''

''He looks perfect,'' Trina said. Her phone rang.

''Please swoon over and answer that,'' Jill said.

Tyler shut the door after she left and walked toward Jill. The look in his eyes made her pulse go haywire. ''Good morning, beautiful,'' he said, and lowered his mouth to hers.

Jill swallowed a moan at the touch of his lips. He kissed her gently but purposefully.

''Miss me?''

''When?'' she asked, indulging herself, for just a few seconds she told herself, in his taste and scent.

''The minute I left you last night,'' he said, rubbing his mouth from side to side over hers.

She felt her knees turn to butter and her nipples tighten. Too much indulgence. She took a careful breath and made the excruciatingly difficult move away from him.

''Miss me?'' he asked again, his gaze falling over her in a warm wave.

''No,'' she insisted for the sake of her sanity.

He shook his head and brushed his knuckles over her aching nipples. ''You're lying.''

She could have denied it again, but she feared her nose would grow like Pinocchio's. He was right. He was getting to her, and she needed to stop him.

Six

Tyler's first press conference was starting and he was nowhere to be found. "Thank you for coming. Dr. Logan will be here shortly," Jill told the crowd and grabbed a house phone to page him.

Moments later he rushed into the room. "Sorry," he told Jill, squeezing her arm. "Is this where I'm supposed to stand?" he asked moving toward the podium."

Jill attached a microphone to his collar. She could see he was distracted. "Problem?"

He shrugged. "Later," he said, then his lips drew upward into a smile that didn't reach his eyes. "What can I do for you nice folks who had the sorry luck to get me as your assignment?"

The crowd laughed. One reporter stepped forward. "How do you feel about your new modeling career?"

"I'm sure it will be brief," Tyler said. "The photographer says I move around too much."

"Seriously," a woman began, "how do you feel about the pediatric cardiology wing?"

"Passionately," Tyler said. "We need it. The kids need it. The parents need it, and the good people of Fort Worth are just the ones to pull together and make something great happen."

"You're not a native of Fort Worth?"

"No, but I've got Cowtown in my blood. I was raised on a ranch in West Texas."

"Dr. Tyler," another woman reporter said, stepping forward, "some of our readers will be interested in your hobbies and favorites."

"I ride a motorcycle. I prefer a horse, but my landlord wouldn't permit it."

The crowd laughed again.

"Your favorite color?"

He glanced at Jill and gave a devil's smile. "Pink." His pager went off amidst the tittering. He looked at Jill and shook his head.

She immediately sensed he had something pressing and stepped forward. "An emergency?"

He nodded grimly.

"Go," she said, and turned back toward the group of reporters. "Dr. Logan is doing what we all want him to do most, and that's take care of his patients. If you have any additional questions, I'll try to answer them. Feel free to use the press kit. The first ad mock-up is also available.''

An hour later she took the elevator up to the floor that housed his patients and found Tyler standing over a bed where a girl lay sleeping and a monitor bleeped her heartbeat. Another nurse stood in the room. Tyler must have felt Jill's presence. He looked up and seemed to drink in her presence.

''Thanks for covering for me with the press,'' he said as he left the room.

''That's my job.''

''You do it well,'' he said.

''As you do yours.''

He pushed his hand through his hair. ''The trouble with my job is that humans perform it, but you can't be human. You have to perform perfectly, because someone's life is at stake.''

''How do you do it?''

''In surgery I never think about anything except the procedure. I don't think about the kid or the parents. But when I finish, that's when I let myself think about the kid.'' His face wrinkled in pain, and he led her out of the room. ''Lilly, that girl in there, has so many problems with her heart it's a miracle she's alive. She's been in for twelve surgeries and I've performed the last two, but she has multiple deformities. Every time she comes in her parents and I know this could be the time her heart just quits. She went into arrest on the table yesterday.''

"Have you ever lost a patient?" Jill asked, feeling the strength of his tension.

"No, and I don't ever want to."

Her heart swelled with emotion for him. "What can I do for you?"

His lips twitched. "Kiss me."

Jill rolled her eyes and turned away. "I'll talk to you later. Hope you get some rest."

"Hey, Jill," he called to her back.

She glanced over her shoulder at him. "What?"

"What did you do with the flowers?"

She refused to give him an ounce of satisfaction in that area. "None of your business."

Her doorbell woke her at 4:00 a.m.

Jill stumbled out of bed, pushed her hands through the sleeves of her robe and went downstairs to the front door. She looked through the peephole, and her heart jumped when she saw Tyler on her front porch.

She whipped open the door immediately, taking in his unshaven face, rumpled clothes and weary eyes. A knot of concern tightened in her chest. "What's wrong?"

"Lilly died."

Jill's heart fell to her feet at the gutted tone of his voice. She couldn't not hold him. Tugging him into her condo, she wrapped her arms around him. "I'm sorry. I'm so sorry."

"She went into arrest three times, and the doctor

on call brought her back two. By the time they called me, she was gone.'' He swore and pulled away, turning his back to her. ''It was the strangest damn thing. I hung around until after midnight. A little over an hour later she went into arrest. It was as if she was waiting for me to leave to die. I should have been there.''

She hated seeing him so torn up. ''You can't always be there.''

''It's my job to be there to take care of a patient in a medical crisis,'' he said, his voice harsh.

''And you did more than that by staying until after midnight.''

''It wasn't enough.''

''You told me she hadn't been expected to live as long as she already had.''

''She shouldn't have died in a damn hospital. She was only eleven. She shouldn't have died period,'' he said.

Jill slowly walked toward him and touched his shoulder. ''Do you think that maybe it was just her time?''

''It is never my patient's time to go,'' he said, his voice clipped.

Jill's eyes widened and she took a careful breath. ''And I thought you were the only doctor I'd met who didn't suffer from a God complex.''

He hung his head. ''I didn't want her to die.''

Jill walked around in front of him and took his face in her hands. ''Of course you didn't. She was lucky to have you for her doctor, to have someone so skilled and so caring. She was very lucky.''

''Not lucky enough.''

''It sounds to me like you helped stretch her time.''

''That's what her parents said.'' His gaze met hers, and she felt herself drowning in her need to help him, if that were possible.

She tugged him to her sofa. ''Sit down. I'll be right back.'' She went to her small stash of liquor, poured a double shot of whisky and returned to set it on the sofa table.

He glanced up at her with a raised eyebrow.

''Drink it.''

''Bossy?''

''Just at 4:00 a.m.,'' she said with a slight smile.

He tossed back the drink, grimaced, swallowed then banged the glass on the table.

''Another?'' she asked, reaching for the glass and refilling it.

He drank the second and looked at her. ''Now what?''

''Now we take off your jacket,'' she said, tugging his leather jacket down his sleeves. ''Then your shoes,'' she said, bending down to pull off his boots.

He met her gaze as she stood. ''Don't stop now.''

She smiled and shook her head. ''Come on.'' She led him up the stairs to her bedroom. ''I don't want to mislead you. We're not going to make love,'' she told him as she unbuttoned his shirt and pushed it off his broad shoulders.

"Why not?" he asked, his eyes dark with a brooding desire.

"Not the right time," she said, feeling her pulse triple as she unfastened his belt. She hesitated before she slowly unzipped his jeans, easing the zipper down over the bulge of his masculinity. Her hands began to tremble. She stopped and swallowed. "I think you can finish taking them off."

Tyler shoved off his jeans, and she took in the sight of his well-muscled tall body. This was going to be more difficult than she'd thought. She was more aroused than she'd planned, but Jill sensed he needed something different, and she was determined to give it to him.

"Lie down on the bed," she said, steeling herself for the moment she would touch him. He shrank the space of the double bed, and she took a breath before she sat on the bed. She lifted her fingers to his brow and stroked his forehead.

His throat worked and his eyes glinted with confusion. "What are you doing?"

She continued to stroke his forehead and eyelids. "Does it feel good?"

"Yes," he said. "But what—"

"Hush," she said, sliding her finger over his mouth. "The doctor takes care of everyone. Every once in a while, someone needs to take care of the doctor. Just relax."

For a moment he looked as if he were going to argue, then he took a deep breath and closed his eyes. Jill continued stroking his face until his breathing grew deep and regular. He was far too handsome for the good of the female race, she thought as she looked down at his chiseled face. Strong brows framed his large eyes crowned with black spiky eyelashes. Crinkles of concentration formed on either side of his eyes, his nose was straight, his chin stubborn and his mouth generous.

Even in sleep, he looked full of vitality. He used his charisma to help the healing process. Perhaps, she thought fancifully, he was the sorcerer.

But not tonight. Tonight he was a man.

Jill felt a stirring sensation in her, almost like the wind before a storm, sweeping across places she'd thought were locked away, slipping into secret places in her soul. Disturbed, she frowned. Comforting Tyler wasn't about sex. It wasn't even about love. It was about simple human compassion and nothing more, she told herself.

Shrugging out of her robe, and lying beside him on the bed, she gently nudged him on his side and held him from behind, her breasts against his back, her arm curled around his waist. Human compassion, her mind mocked her, as Tyler folded his hand over hers.

Tyler awakened to the sensation of slim, feminine legs entwined with his. Her breasts teased his back.

Small puffs of breath tickled his neck. He couldn't recall a nicer hug even though this one was backward. He couldn't recall a woman being so tender with him since he was a child. He might have smiled if not for the small, slim hand riding dangerously low on his abdomen. But that was Jill's hand, and the knowledge that she was so close fully aroused him. He bit back a groan.

She snuggled and her hand slid another inch closer. Tyler grew warm. To have her this close was heaven. And hell. He could slowly roll over and take her mouth, kiss her awake, take her breasts in his palms, then slide his hands down her ribs and abdomen and lower. He would explore her with his fingers and his tongue until she awakened wet and wanting him. Then he would slide inside her and pump.

Unable to stand it any longer, he carefully rolled over and slid his fingers through her tousled hair. Her cheeks were pink in sleep, her lips slightly parted as if she were waiting for his kiss. That was enough for Tyler.

He lowered his mouth to hers. She nuzzled against him and sighed. He increased the pressure and she stretched her arms around him. She was so sweet, so sexy, and he wanted her so much. Rolling onto his back, he pulled her on top of him and relished the sensation of every inch of her body pressed against his.

She moaned, then pulled her head slightly back.

"What—" She blinked and sighed. "What are you doing?"

"Kissing you," he said, taking her mouth again.

She started to respond, then pulled back. "This isn't a good idea," she said in a husky voice.

"I think it's a great way to wake up. I think we should do it more often."

She pushed her hair from her face and tried to slide away, but he stopped her. "Don't rush off," he said. "You lured me to your bed last night. You're not going to leave me all alone now, are you?"

"I told you we weren't going to—"

"Make love?" He grinned, lifting his hand to stroke her hair. "That was last night."

"Last night was an act of human kindness," she insisted, pushing off him. "I realize you have a one-track mind at times, but you needed something different."

"Whisky and Jill to watch over me," he said, raising himself up on his elbow. He reached for her hand. "Don't pull away," he said. "Thank you."

She bit her lip and glanced away self-consciously. "It wasn't much. It was just—"

He tugged her closer. "It was a lot. More than anyone else has done for me in my adult life."

"Maybe because you seem so self-sufficient, so self-contained," she said.

"Like you," he said.

Her head moved up in surprise.

"Takes one to know one," he said with a slight grin, feeling the connection between them strengthen. He followed his instincts. "I'd like you to move in with me the rest of your time that you're here in Fort Worth."

Her eyes widened and her jaw worked. "Pardon?"

"I want you to move in with me," he said.

She shook her head. "I don't think that's a good idea."

"It's a great idea. We can be together and answer our questions."

Jill wondered if she was going to have a panic attack. She pulled her hand away. "It would be like opening Pandora's box."

He sat up, looking entirely too seductive, entirely too right in her bed, as if he belonged there. "Jill, if you didn't feel something for me, you would have thrown my rear end out of here."

Feeling as if she'd just drunk five cups of coffee, she stood. "I told you that was about human kindness."

"Completely impersonal," he said.

She started to nod, but hesitated. "Well, it wasn't completely impersonal."

"You're not attracted to me at all?"

"I didn't say that. You're not an ugly man," she said, growing more uneasy by the second. He should be wearing more clothes. He shouldn't be on her bed.

"Have you always run from something you might like?" he asked.

"I don't run," she corrected, but grabbed her robe and wrapped it around her. "I try to avoid things that might be bad for me."

Unruffled by her nervousness, he reclined on her bed as if he owned it. His mouth lifted in a maddening, sexy grin. "You're not saying I'm bad, are you?"

She picked up his jeans and tossed them at him. "Very bad. Get dressed. Get gone."

He made a tsking sound and slowly rose. "You need to learn more about our Texas hospitality. You'd learn in no time by living with me."

She held out his shirt to him. "I'm sure you'd teach me more than manners," she muttered under her breath.

He took his shirt and her hand, pulling her to him. His gaze made her heart flip-flop. "Jill, you can run, but you can't hide. Some things are inevitable."

That afternoon Trina brought in another bouquet of flowers.

"Oh, no," Jill said. "I'm going to have to call him and—"

"It's a different florist. Maybe they're from someone new."

Jill wrinkled her brow in confusion and reached for the card. "I can't imagine who—"

Thank you for last night. Tyler

Jill felt heat rise to her cheeks.

Trina smiled. "Well?" she prompted. "Is it someone new?"

"They, uh—"

Tyler burst into the room. "Ah, you got them," he said, nodding toward the flowers. "Thank you again for last night."

Trina's eyes grew as large as golf balls. "Dr. Logan," she said surprised and envious. She looked at Jill. "Last night? My goodness. I thought—"

"It's not the way it looks," Jill quickly said, thinking of the hospital grapevine. "Or sounds. Dr. Logan was upset and came to my condo last night."

Trina lifted her hand and shook her head. "Oh, you don't have to tell me any more." She backed out of the office, giving Tyler a wistful glance. "I really understand."

"No," Jill said, but Trina closed the door.

Jill turned back to Tyler. "Within three minutes it will be all over the hospital that we're sleeping together."

He grinned. "We did."

"Yes, but—" She broke off in frustration. "Tyler, why did you have to do this?"

"You don't like them? You liked the ones from Gordie well enough." He leaned across her desk. "Besides, isn't it polite for me to thank you?"

"Yes, but—" She sighed, remembering her own manners. "Thank you. They're lovely, and it was thoughtful of you."

"You're welcome. Change your mind about moving in with me?"

"No," she said.

"Well, keep tonight open," he said.

"I may be busy writing some radio spots," she told him, thinking she needed some breathing room from Tyler for her sanity.

"Not tonight. Time for another field trip," he told her.

"Not to the ranch," she said.

"No. A Fort Worth landmark. Important for your education of our fine city."

"I appreciate your kindness, but—"

He shook his head. "This is part of the barter for my modeling services."

"I thought the trip to the ranch covered that."

"Oh, no," he said. "That was just the first installment."

Seven

The money for the wing was rolling in already. The billboards were up, articles had begun to appear in statewide press, and it looked as though a lot of Texans wanted to be part of the heart menders' posse.

Jill had no idea how to dress for this field trip, so she slipped on a pair of black jeans and the only Western-style blouse she owned. She stepped into a pair of boots and the doorbell rang.

She opened it to Tyler who was wearing aviator sunglasses at dusk.

"What's with the shades?" she asked.

"It was either that or buy a wig," he grumbled, strolling into her condo and taking them off. "Do you have any idea how many people have already seen the billboards?''

Jill smiled. "Ohh, a celebrity already, huh?"

He bared his teeth in a nonsmile. "Something like that. It means I need a disguise and a bodyguard when I go out in public." Then he really smiled. "I want you to guard my body."

Jill rolled her eyes at the same time her skin warmed at the expression in his eyes. "What an invitation," she said. "Why me? I'm sure you can find any number of women who would be happy to guard your body day and—"

"I want you," he said, looking dead serious. "I don't want any number of women. I want you."

Her heart stuttered. His words had more impact than a kiss. "I, uh—" She swallowed and changed the subject. "I didn't know how to dress for the field trip. I imagine it could be anything from a hayride to a rodeo."

"No hayride," he said, his gaze falling over her, warming her. "You look good to me."

As he did to her. Good and *so* bad for her.

The noise of Billy Bob's dance hall hit her like a punch the second she and Tyler walked through the door. She looked at Tyler. "This is the field trip?" she said loudly as they walked past video games, pool tables, slot machines and throngs and throngs of people. She noticed an indoor rodeo ring, trophy animals on the walls and a glittering saddle hanging from the ceiling like a disco ball.

"I wanted you to experience some local color," he said, his lips twitching as he put on his aviator sunglasses.

"This is definitely colorful."

"Ready to two-step?"

"I don't know how," she admitted, gazing at the sea of dancers.

"It's easy," he said, taking her by the hand to the dance floor. "I'll show you."

His nearness immediately upset her equilibrium. His hand was strong in hers, his other firmly guiding her hip. As an old George Strait tune played, she tried to focus on his instructions. She stepped on his foot. "Sorry," she muttered, then stepped on his other foot. "Are you sure this is a good idea? I'm not sure I'm cowgirl material."

He chuckled. "Sure you are," he said. "I like the fringe," he told her sweeping an index finger over the fringed yoke of her shirt, dangerously close to her breast.

Jill held her breath. She couldn't see the expression in his eyes because he still wore the sunglasses.

The music shifted to a slow tune that didn't require the two-step. He wrapped his arms around her waist and pulled her closer.

Jill felt the beat of his heart against her chest as if it matched her own. Despite her clumsiness, despite the fact that she could never see herself as a Texan, despite all the reasons it should feel wrong, it felt so right to be held by him. Jill hadn't danced, hadn't been held in years, and the combination of the twangy romantic song and Tyler brought tears to her eyes.

One of his legs slid between hers, and he pressed the small of her back so that her pelvis curved into his. "Look at me," he told her, nuzzling her forehead.

She wanted to soak in his scent and vibrancy. She wanted to absorb his very essence. She wanted to touch his face and kiss him. She wanted to see his eyes. "I miss your eyes," she whispered. The words were out of her mouth before she could stop them.

He immediately flipped the glasses up on his head, and the unadulterated wanting in his gaze rocked her world. "So you like my eyes?" he asked, and dipped his mouth to briefly brush her temple. She wondered how a normally chaste move could feel so sexual.

"Is there anything else you like about me?" he asked against her ear.

Jill shivered. *Too much,* she thought. She liked *too much* about him. His thighs brushed hers, and she felt his hardness against her, showing her in no uncertain terms how much he wanted her.

"Nothing?" he said with a rough chuckle. "Well, there's a lot I like about you. I like," he told her as he brushed a finger over her hair, "the way your hair feels against my skin. I'd like to feel it on more of my skin."

Her brain was a jumble. "Maybe it's the conditioner I use," she managed.

He shook his head. "I like the way your eyes hint at your secrets."

"They don't do that, do they?"

He nodded slowly. "Yeah, they say you want me."

Exasperated, Jill pulled his shades from his head and covered her own eyes with them.

He chuckled again. "I like your stubborn, snooty nose."

"That doesn't sound like a compliment."

"I like your mouth," he said, briefly brushing his mouth against hers. "I'd like to spend a lot of time on your mouth."

He rubbed his index finger down her throat to the opening of her blouse, dipping it just inside to the top of her breast. "I like the way your skin feels."

"When are you going to stop trying to seduce me?" she asked over the loud hammer of her heart.

"No time in the near future. Is it working?"

She wanted to say no, but the lie stuck in her throat. It was hard to deny, when she wished there were no clothes between them and she wished they weren't dancing with so many other people around. It was hard to deny, when she was beginning to feel such a sense of fate about him.

She felt a vibrating buzz from his hip to hers.

He swore and looked down at his pager. The vibration was his pager, she realized, and was so embarrassed she was glad she wore his glasses.

"It's the hospital. I'm on call, so I need to check in." He kissed her quickly and tugged her off the dance floor as he headed for a pay phone.

She wondered how he could switch gears so quickly from seductive arousal to doctor mode. Her head was still muddy from dancing with him. He pushed a couple of coins in a phone and dialed. She heard him echo something about a three-year-old and an automobile accident where the mother was dead on arrival. She felt as if she'd been plunged into ice water.

"Gotta go," he said, completely focused after he hung up. "I can run you home if we do it quickly. The kid's scared to death, and they're having problems with him. There's no next of kin. ER discovered a heart problem when they examined him. He'll probably need surgery after some tests."

She shook her head. "I don't want you to take the time," she said. "I'll get a ride from someone else at the hospital."

"Sorry," he said, his touch regretful as they moved toward the exit.

"This is important," she said, and asked because she had to know. "The mother died, didn't she?"

He narrowed his eyes and nodded. "Yep."

The situation wasn't identical, but as they drove the short distance to the hospital in tense silence, she wondered if he was thinking about his mother's death. She couldn't help remembering her own devastating accident.

Walking with him into the emergency room, she felt a sense of foreboding. Or was it fate? Even though she smelled it every day, tonight the hospital's antiseptic scent made her stomach clench. Tonight somebody's mommy had died. The hushed, worried voices of patients waiting to be treated took on an air of unreality.

She thought about the boy, the orphan, and how terrified he must be. She remembered her own terror. She thought of Tyler's terror at losing his mother so many years ago.

"Are you okay?" Tyler asked, bringing her back to the present. "You look pale."

"I'm okay," she said, wanting to be okay, willing herself to be okay.

"I can try to find you a ride," he began.

She shook her head. "I think I'll hang around here for a little while." She hesitated, then went with her instinct. "If the boy needs someone to hold his hand, let me know."

His eyes flickered in surprise, and he cocked his head to one side. "Are you sure?"

She nodded.

"Okay. I'll let you know. Thanks for the dance."

"For stepping on your feet," she said.

"More field trips," he said, and quickly kissed her. "Later."

Jill went up to her office and made coffee and

sketched out some press releases. She paced back and forth, turned on her sound machine and made doodles until Tyler called her.

"You know that offer you made earlier?" he asked. "Is it still good?"

"Yes," she said, her stomach a jumble of nerves.

"I have a buddy named Sam here, and I think he could use some female companionship."

She felt that same overwhelming mix of foreboding and fate, but didn't fight it. "I'll be right up."

"Are you sure?" he asked.

"Yes."

Jill didn't know why she felt so strongly about this situation and this child. She just knew she couldn't turn away from it or him. When she saw him, dark curly hair, huge, frightened dark eyes and wearing a cast on his right arm, sobbing uncontrollably in the social worker's arms, her heart broke.

Tyler walked to her side wearing a weary expression on his face. "We've been through three nurses and the social worker. If you've got any magic, we sure could use it."

She approached the toddler and held out her hands. "I'll take him."

Jill held him in a rocking chair, and Sam continued to cry for several minutes. She stroked his forehead and his eyes and told him he was going to be okay. His cries for his mother wrenched at her, but she continued to softly touch his face, the way she would have soothed her own child if she'd had the chance, the way she had soothed a grown man.

Sam's cries turned to hiccups, and he sighed.

"Would you like some juice?" she whispered.

He popped his forefinger in his mouth and stared at her, sniffing.

"Juice?" she asked again.

He nodded, and Tyler caught her eye, then called a nurse. The juice promptly appeared, and Sam sipped it noisily through a straw. Halfway through, he began to cry again.

Tyler lifted his head. "You want me to get some-one else?"

"No," she said, determined to stay with him. Someone needed to. "I'd cry, too, if I were him. Could you bring me some books?"

He nodded.

She rocked Sam more and sang silly songs. He took breaks from his crying to stare at her. She read a book and he quieted, so she read a second one and a third, a fourth, and during the fifth book, prayer, exhaustion or a combination of the two won, and Sam fell asleep.

"Want me to put him to bed?"

She shook her head. "He'll be frightened when he wakes up."

"You can't stay here all night," he said.

She glanced up from the sleeping child. "Why not? It's Friday. I wouldn't have worked tomorrow, anyway."

"You don't have to do this, Jill," he said.

She gave a wry smile. Sometime during the past hours she'd faced another waterloo, and this time she'd won. "I think I do."

His face lit with recognition, and he nodded slowly. "He needs surgery. His mother was a un-wed teenager with no insurance. No next of kin, no nothing. I've asked the directors to use the first of the heart menders' posse money for Sam's medical expenses."

"Excellent use of the money," she said, resting her head on the back of her chair and closing her eyes. She felt Tyler's gaze on her.

"You're a brave woman," he said.

"I'm a wimp about some things," she admitted because it was late and she couldn't summon her tough-lady attitude at the moment.

"Not tonight," he said, his voice a caress.

"I was just persistent," she said around a yawn. "Persistence solves a lot of problems. When do you think you'll perform his surgery?"

"Maybe as early as Sunday."

She nodded and opened her eyes to meet Tyler's gaze. "He might have been unlucky to lose his mother, but he's lucky to have you for his doctor."

"If you keep saying things like that you'll make my head swell," he told her, "and other parts, too."

She couldn't fight Tyler tonight. She just didn't have it in her. "I'm not saying anything that isn't true."

He leaned closer and ran his fingers through a strand of her hair. "When I look at you, I want you so bad I can taste it. Tell me I'm not in this alone."

His intensity made her stomach tighten. "I want you," she admitted, "in a way that frightens me."

Over the next forty-eight hours she astonished him with her tenacity and perseverance. Sam awakened crying for his mother, and Jill comforted him. She sang songs and read books until her voice grew hoarse. Although he tried to get her to go home, she refused and took brief rests on a cot he brought into Sam's room. It wasn't that she always knew the perfect remedy for Sam. If there was a magic it was, as she'd said, her persistence. Throughout the hours, he watched the two of them bond like warriors in a battle.

Despite the demons that must have haunted her, she seemed to grow stronger with each passing moment, assuring Sam that someone would take care of him. He wondered if this was her trial by fire, if this was the reason she'd taken his dare.

By Sunday noon Sam's surgery was complete. He awakened quickly in recovery, and Jill came to his side. She stayed there until late Sunday night, and Tyler insisted she go home.

"I don't want him to wake up and panic," she argued, but the dark circles under her eyes spoke louder.

"You can't be here every single time he wakes

up,'' Tyler told her. ''It's physically impossible. You've gotten him through the worst weekend of his life. He has to be able to let other people take care of him.''

She sighed and stood unsteadily.

Concern raced through him. He swore. ''You're so exhausted I'm almost afraid to drive you home on my bike.''

''Oh, I'll be okay.'' But she was swaying as she said it.

He put his hands on her slim shoulders. ''Give the nurse some pointers, then we're leaving.''

She sighed again and rubbed her eyes, walking to the nurses' station. ''Whatever you do, don't lose the bunny. He loves *The Little Engine That Could* and the song 'Mares Eat Oats.' Do you know it?''

The nurse shook her head, so in the middle of the hallway, in a croaky voice, Jill sang the silly song, and turned him inside out.

He knew he didn't want her for just a night. It couldn't be forever, he told himself. Nothing ever was. The Logan Curse taunted him, and he felt the familiar twitch of his eye. When it came to love, Logan men didn't win. He scowled. He didn't believe in the curse, but he also didn't believe he would ever know what forever felt like.

He was determined, however, to make Jill Hershey his for whatever time they could have.

Jill was numb. She was pleased with herself that she hadn't fallen off Tyler's motorcycle. The bath he'd drawn for her had taken what little starch was left in her limbs. The scented water was beginning to cool. Loath to leave the tub, she knew she needed to go to bed.

Her only trouble was that her legs didn't want to help. She tried unsuccessfully to rise from the tub and only succeeded in dropping back down, splashing cold water on herself.

"Jill?" Tyler called. "Are you okay?"

Embarrassed beyond belief, she called back, "Fine. Just fine."

She tried again, but her legs were still no use. "This is so embarrassing."

Tyler must have heard her pitiful efforts. "I'm coming in."

Panic crowded her throat. "No!" she squeaked.

Too late. He stared down at her. She closed her eyes. She'd practiced the same thing as a child. If she couldn't see him, then he couldn't see her.

"What's wrong?"

"My legs are spaghetti. Beyond al dente." She could feel the blush of her life building from her toes. "Just go back out and give me a minute or two and—"

The sensation of his arms under her back and legs as he picked her up stopped her words and heart and forced her eyes open. "You have no idea how awkward this is for me."

"I've seen many naked bodies," he assured her.

"Why don't I feel better?" she asked.

"I'm a doctor. I've seen many bodies," he said, "and yours is very nice. Is that a birthmark on your left breast?"

"Stop looking," she told him.

He chuckled, grabbed a towel and carried her to her bed. She saw a cup of kava tea on her nightstand and a nightgown. In the same way he would care for a child, he pulled the gown over her head and offered her the tea.

She sipped it, feeling his gaze on her. "It would be easier for me if you would be less kind."

Arms crossed over his chest, he stood over her looking confused. "Why?"

"Because I don't want to like you." She made a face and shook her head. "I already like you. I don't want to fall for you. I don't want to think you have the capacity for a deep relationship with me. I don't want to get any crazy ideas that I could really be special to you."

His eyes made sensual promises that he would keep at another time. He took the cup of tea from her hands and tucked her in. He flicked off the lamp, brushed his lips over her cheek and whispered, "That wouldn't be crazy at all."

Eight

A kiss wasn't going to rouse this Sleeping Beauty, Tyler decided the next morning as he looked at Jill. The woman had not changed position the entire night.

He had wanted to make love to her every day since she had arrived at the hospital, but last night he had wanted her so much it had kept him awake half the night. Now he knew she wanted him and was frightened by it. He just had to make the desire stronger than the fear.

Leaning against the doorjamb, he shook his head. Nope, a kiss was not going to cut it this morning. He would need to bring out the big guns.

French toast.

He threw in extra cinnamon to help his cause and halfway through the second batch on the griddle, she appeared in the doorway. "This is a dream," she said in a sleep-husky voice. "You can cook, too."

"Nothing gourmet," he said. "But I get tired of takeout and frozen food sometimes."

She reached for the phone.

"Sam is fine," he told her. "He woke up whimpering for 'Jelly,' but the rabbit, the book, and the oat song and a promise to see 'Jelly' later quieted him.

She sighed and gave a little smile. "Thanks for checking."

"He's my patient, too."

Her smile broadened. "I like the way you're possessive about your patients."

"I can be possessive about other things, too," he said, which was as much a surprise to Tyler as it might be to Jill. Tyler had never been possessive about a woman before, but he could easily see himself becoming that way about Jill. "Powdered sugar or syrup?" he asked, flipping the toast from the griddle onto a plate.

She bit her lip sheepishly. "Both."

His lips twitched. "Indulgent little thing, aren't you? Are you sure you don't want ice cream and hot-fudge sauce too?"

She lifted her hand. "Don't mention ice cream.

Because ice cream goes with everything. Everything," she emphasized.

Tyler bit his tongue and bided his time, telling himself that very soon he would be consuming her like a bowl of ice cream.

"How am I different from your stupid ex-husband?" he asked as she poured orange juice for both of them.

She looked surprised, then thoughtful. "You are dark and he is blond. He is a salesman. You are, too, but not professional. You just use your persuasive abilities when it serves your cause, and your cause is a good one. He is a flirt. You are too, but—" She frowned.

"But what?"

"I don't know," she shrugged. "Your way is different, somehow." She grew serious. "You are excellent in crisis situations. You aren't the type to fall apart when others may be depending on you."

She didn't need to finish by saying that her husband hadn't cut the mustard during a crisis. Tyler had an agenda for asking the question—reduce the fear.

She ate another bite of toast and looked at him consideringly, seeming to hesitate. "You also seem to be more—" She hesitated, a self-conscious expression washing over her face. "—sexually driven."

"Does that bother you?" he asked mildly.

"No," she said too quickly. "Why should it bother me? It doesn't really affect me."

"I don't affect you at all, right?"

"I, uh, didn't say that," she hedged, and took a sip of orange juice.

"How long do you think it's been since I've had sex with anyone besides myself?"

She squirmed in her seat. "I really don't know. No idea," she said.

"Take a guess."

"I really—" She exhaled. "A week or two, maybe three."

"Try a year."

Her jaw dropped.

"Sex can be a pretty combustible action. Not just physically, but mentally and emotionally. You have to be careful with yourself and other people."

"A year?" she echoed. "But you're so—"

"So what?"

"So sexy. Everything about you. The way you walk, the way you talk, the way you smell. And women pine after you."

"I'm careful," he said, deliberately holding her gaze. "I want it to be right." He could tell he was shaking up her perception of him, slicing past her objections. Good, he thought. He leaned closer and took her mouth in a surprise kiss. She tasted of sugar and orange juice. He cupped her chin and felt his need for her rise in his chest like an ache. He was beginning to wonder if they could make the ache go away.

Jill spent the afternoon in a state of complete distraction. She tried to blame it on her lack of sleep and concern for Sam, but she was truly thinking about Tyler. Flowers arrived while she was pacing her office and brooding over him.

Trina raised her eybrows. "It's the *other* florist," she said.

Jill made a face. At least Tyler wasn't here to witness it. She reached for the card, and he blew into her office.

Jill swore under her breath. She'd experienced the choreography for this scene one too many times.

Tyler frowned at the flowers. "I'm beginning to not like this guy."

"He's a very nice person. I think he just doesn't seem to grasp subtlety very well," she said weakly.

"I'll say," Trina agreed. "Do you want to keep them or share?"

"Share."

Trina promptly removed the offending bouquet from the office while Tyler steamed in front of her.

"I think I may have to call him."

"Good idea," he said. "Unless you're interested in him."

"No," she said. "I mean, he's a very nice man, very stable, but—"

"But he doesn't crank your engine, flip your

switch, light your fire, get you going,'' he said, his gaze dropping over her like a hot breeze.

Her heart tripped over itself as he moved closer. ''Uh, no.''

He backed her against her desk. ''How long has it been since you had sex, Jill?''

She swallowed. ''I told you. A long time.'' She tried to take a breath, but couldn't seem to find it.

He brushed his body against hers. ''I'm gonna change that answer very soon, but you'll come to me,'' he told her, and took her mouth.

It wasn't a nice little kiss. It was a hungry, sexual oath of more to come. He meant business, and her body responded like kindling to a match. He slid his hands down to cup her bottom and pull her against him to feel his arousal.

She had the exhilarating and terrifying sense that he would take her at this moment on her desk. She had the exhilarating and terrifying sense that she would let him.

He pulled back instead, and the passion in his eyes was almost too much for her to bear. They had been through so much together during the past few days it was as if their bodies were demanding an ultimate union.

Trina opened the door and Tyler quickly turned around shielding Jill from her prying eyes. ''Dr. Logan, I don't mean to bother you, but there's a discrepancy on your favorite color, and a reporter from a West Texas weekly newspaper would like to clarify. It's a human-interest story.''

Tyler glanced back at Jill's dress and met her gaze with brief possessiveness. ''Purple,'' he said, and headed for the door.

Trina blinked, then slowly nodded at his departure. ''Okay.''

That evening Jill visited with Sam, reading, singing and playing. She marveled at his resilience. It was hard to believe he'd just lost his mother and had been through major surgery. He was still quiet, and Social Services was searching for a foster family who could handle children with special needs, but he smiled shyly a few times and hugged her tightly.

The sensation of his little body grabbing on to her neck twisted her heart and made her long for the child she would never bear. She didn't, however, feel the same overwhelming grief anymore. The loss was still present, but taking care of Sam this past weekend had changed her. Odd, but caring for him nonstop had done something to her. She might often feel a twinge about babies, but she would never avoid children or their causes in the future. She wouldn't deny herself the fulfillment and pleasure.

As Sam drifted off to sleep, she thought of Tyler and a different sort of fulfillment and pleasure she'd also avoided for years. She groaned.

Putting Sam to bed, she remembered Tyler's

claim this afternoon—that she would come to him. She still couldn't believe he'd said that.

Jill had never gone to a man's house with the intention to seduce. She didn't know if she had the nerve. While Tyler's sensuality was like a tornado, hers was like an ocean breeze.

How could she go to his apartment? She didn't even know his address. It wouldn't be difficult to find, she thought. But what would she wear? What would she say? What would she do?

Agitated, she left Sam's room. She had no idea how to seduce Tyler. Sex with her husband hadn't been particularly memorable. She suspected her experience with Tyler might be quite different.

How could she go? she wondered, swearing under her breath. How could she not?

It took her hours to get up the nerve, and she looked at it six ways from Sunday and came up with six different answers. She picked up a bottle of wine and a country CD at a quick mart and found her way to his apartment. His motorcycle was parked out front.

She cut her engine and reconsidered for the fiftieth time, then gathered her courage. Or was it insanity? She walked to his front door and knocked before she could think about it.

It took him such a long time to answer she almost left.

He answered the door in a pair of jeans with the

top button undone and no shirt. His hair was mussed and his eyelids heavy. He'd been sleeping.

Jill felt her embarrassment reach epic proportions. Thank goodness he couldn't see her face because of the darkness. "I'm sorry. It's too late. You've been sleeping," she said without taking a breath. "I shouldn't have come."

He reached out and took her wrist. "No," he said. "I was just dozing. Come in."

He pulled the door shut behind her and stood there for a long moment watching her in the semi-darkness.

Jill had practiced a zippy little speech that evaporated from her mind the second she stared at his bare chest. Just the right amount of chest hair arrowed down to the top of his jeans. Her pulse clamored in her head.

Forcing her gaze away from him, she took in what she could of his den. A comfortable couch, a southwestern throw, pillows, an overstuffed chair, a table topped with books and a terra-cotta lamp and an entertainment center.

CD player.

The sight jogged her memory, but her courage sagged. She wanted to say, help! "Are you sure this isn't too late?" she asked in a near whisper.

He shook his head.

"I brought some wine," she said, not quite meeting his gaze. "And a CD. I thought you maybe could give me another lesson in two-stepping." She took a breath. "But you're probably too tired for that, so—"

"I'm not," he said, and reached for the bag she held. He took her hand, too, as if he knew she might back out, and led her to a small kitchen.

"You saw Sam tonight," he said, as he uncorked the wine.

Sam. An easier subject. She took a breath. "Yes. He was doing wonderfully. I think he had more energy than I did," she said.

Tyler filled one wineglass. "His prognosis is excellent. You should feel good. You helped him through a terrible time."

"He kinda helped me, too."

He nodded and offered her a sip.

She took two. "You aren't going to have any?"

"We can share," he said and took the bottle and CD with him as he led her back to the den. "Take off your shoes," he said, and with a slow wicked smile added, "and anything else you might like to ditch."

She stepped out of her shoes, shoved them out of the way and took another gulp of wine. He programmed the CD player, and the music flowed through the room. He took her hand and stood in dance position as if he didn't know she was here to make love with him. His shoulder was warm and muscular beneath her palm, and that single button at the top of his jeans was still unfastened. She bit her lip.

"The secret is the slide. When I slide forward, you slide backward. Slide, slide," he said, beginning the dance. "That's right."

Looking at him clouded her mind, so Jill stared down at her feet and concentrated on the movements.

"Look at me," he said.

"I can't," she said. "You're too distracting."

"That's part of the dance, though. You have to be able to do it even when you're distracted."

"Okay." She looked up and focused just past his shoulder to a picture on the wall.

He chuckled. "You're cheating," he said. "You're not looking at me. This is a social dance. Look at me, Jill."

Hearing him say her name did wonderful things to her respiratory system. "They're your feet," she warned him crisply, and looked into his eyes. She immediately stumbled.

"Slide, slide," he said, holding her gaze.

Clinging to him with her arms, with her eyes, she somehow managed to keep pace.

"Very good. You're ready for the next distraction," he said, and lowered his mouth to hers.

He made the room spin, but she kept dancing. He made love to her mouth, French kissing her, sliding his tongue over hers. *Slide, slide.* His tongue swept into her mouth, his lips seducing her, turning up her body heat.

With his mouth still fastened to hers, he tugged

the zipper of her purple sheath all the way down her back. He pulled her to a stop and sent the dress down over her shoulders and hips to the floor and guided her out of it.

Sweeping her body against his, he skimmed his hands over her bare skin, hair, neck and back as if he couldn't touch enough of her at once. Through the sheer fabric of her bra, his chest abraded her nipples. Jill felt a drugging eroticism seep through her.

"You feel so good," he said, teasing the underside of her breast with his thumb.

She felt her bra snap loose, and he toyed with the stiff tips of her breasts. The sensation made her restless; she pushed her breast against his palm. Too much, not enough. He must have felt her urgency. Seconds later he was pushing her stockings down her legs. She stepped out of them and felt his palms cupping her buttocks, then his fingers sliding between her thighs to find her wet and wanting. Jill had never experienced such a powerful rush of raw need. Sensation after sensation washed over her. The scent of his need, the sound of his breath mingled with hers, the feeling of his denim-clad leg brushing between her bare legs.

He swore. "Jill, we just started and I already know I can't get enough of you." He devoured her mouth and touched her secret places with his fingers, turning her femininity into a passionflower. Her bare skin felt sunburned. She wanted him closer, as close as he could be. The razor edge of sexual desperation startled her. She glided her hands over the corded muscles of his back, his broad shoulders and the soft hair on his hard chest. She dropped her mouth to his throat, and the open button of his jeans taunted her.

"Why," she demanded in a voice husky to her own ears, "am I naked while you're still dressed?"

"Because as soon as these jeans are off, I'm going to be inside you," he said roughly.

She hoped that was a promise. Feeling more wanton and driven than she'd ever dreamed, she eased his zipper down over his bulging masculinity. When he protested, she pressed her mouth to his and slid her hand inside his jeans to cup his full hardness.

He let out a hiss of breath and squeezed her arms. "What are you doing?"

She skimmed her open mouth over his chest. "You don't like it?" she asked, and rubbed her thumb over the moist tip of him.

He growled, lifting her high in his arms and urging her thighs around him. He took one of her swollen breasts into his mouth and drew on her nipple.

Jill gasped, feeling the tug in her nether regions.

"I want in you," he said, swinging her around in his arms and carrying her upstairs.

Her very existence seemed to whirl and spin as he carried her through his bedroom door and eased her down onto his large bed. His eyes glowing like fire, he reached inside the bedside table drawer and pulled out a plastic packet. "I need to protect you."

Jill bit her lip, the bittersweet reality cutting through their passion. "That's taken care of," she said. His gaze falling over her like a desperado staring at gold, he followed her down and began to devour her with his hands and mouth. He dragged his tongue down her neck and chest to her turgid nipple, then kissed his way down her abdomen to her thighs where he took her with his tongue.

The sensation of his tongue on her most sensitive place made her cry out. She climaxed up and over.

With one sure stroke, he thrust inside her taking her to the top again. With fluid, rippling movements, he pumped and she squeezed him intimately.

He closed his eyes as if the pleasure was too much. "I knew you would send me out of control," he muttered, and stiffened from a long unbridled release. Tyler sank to his side and pulled Jill against him. The silence in the room was deafening to her. She felt as if bombs had just exploded around her, inside her. She looked at the man who caused the explosion and wondered if she would ever be the same again.

Nine

Throughout the night Tyler made love to Jill again and again. By morning her body ached in sensitive places, and for the first time in her life she understood the expression "making love until your brains fall out." As she gazed at Tyler's face, she felt distinctly brainless.

She also felt as if Tyler had reached inside her and changed her mind, body and soul, and that frightened her. The power of their passion stunned her. Heaven help her, she'd never experienced anything near it with her husband.

But Tyler didn't believe in forever; Jill wouldn't be staying in Fort Worth forever, anyway; and the mere thought of forever shouldn't be entering her brain.

A sliver of apprehension slid through her. She was beginning to think that she shouldn't have done this. More than her hormones were involved. Of course more than her hormones were involved, or she wouldn't have gotten involved with Tyler in the first place.

She looked at Tyler, who lay there sleeping in all his indolently nude male beauty, and she felt a rush of desire. She closed her eyes. She should not be feeling this. She should not want him again. Goodness, they'd spent the entire night feasting on each other. Her mind, which she was certain had been parked in neutral, started to race.

Maybe it would be best if she left, so she could start thinking straight, because she clearly didn't think straight in his presence. Carefully sliding to the edge of the bed, she got one foot on the floor and Tyler's hand shot out to capture her wrist.

His eyelids fluttered open to reveal his laser-blue eyes, which made her feel as if she were stuck going up the down elevator. "Where are you going?"

"Bathroom," she said.

"Don't be gone long," he said.

She wouldn't, she thought. Just maybe a week or so, if she could find her clothes. She crept downstairs as quietly as she could and felt her face flame at the way her clothes were scattered throughout the den. She tugged on her dress and stepped into her shoes when she couldn't find her stockings.

"Keys," she muttered nervously under her

breath, raking her hand through her hair as she scanned the den. "Purse."

"Kitchen counter," Tyler said.

Jill's heart rose to her throat. She glanced up the stairs to find Tyler nude and watching her.

"Morning-after jitters?" he asked, arching his brow.

She swallowed. "I, uh, started thinking."

"Oh." He made a tsking sound. "You shouldn't do that on an empty stomach."

"Tyler," she said, trying to focus on his ear, "I'm not sure last night was the best—"

"It wasn't the best?" he said in disbelief.

Well, she certainly couldn't say it hadn't been the best. Her nerves bounced in her stomach. "I meant to say it might not have been the best *idea* for us to get involved," she said, and added in a low voice, "intimately."

He walked toward her, his eyes serious. "Too late now."

She took a deep breath and willed her heart to calm down. "Too late for last night, but not for the future."

He looked at her incredulously. She might even say he was hurt if such a thing were possible, and it surely couldn't be. "You wanted a one-night stand?"

Jill cringed. "No! But I didn't expect—" She shook her head. "I had no idea—" She closed her eyes. "It was too much. I can't—" She heard her voice quaver and wanted to swear. "I don't think we should do this again."

"Why?" he demanded.

She opened her eyes and stared at him in exasperation. "Because."

"Has sex ever been that good for you before?"

"No," she admitted. "But—"

"Has it ever been so powerful, so overwhelming—"

She held up her hand. "Stop. I don't know what I expected, but I didn't expect to feel this way. I'm sorry, but I need to find my sanity." Her voice broke, and she bit her lip. "I need to find me. I can't be with you right now. I'm sorry."

She turned on her heel to gather her purse and leave. Just before she closed the door behind her, she heard him say, "You're running, Jill."

A tear squeezed out of the corner of her eye. He might be right, she thought, but she still closed the door behind her and fled to her car.

Tyler licked his wounds. He would never have believed it possible, but a woman had hurt his feelings in a big way. He had just spent the most incredible night in his life making love to the most incredible woman, and she'd said it was a mistake.

Her words left a bitter taste in his mouth and a heaviness to his heart. In the back of his mind the Logan Curse taunted him. His eye twitched at the thought. It couldn't be, he told himself. He didn't believe in it, and he would never put himself in a position where it could be exercised. And he sure as hell wouldn't now.

He showered, went to the hospital and avoided Jill the entire day. If she couldn't see how good they were for each other, then she was blind. The extra attention he was getting because of his billboard exposure did little to salve his ego or hurt. In fact, it irritated him that so many women were interested in him, but not the one who kept taking up space in his head.

The following day he continued to avoid Jill, but halfway through, he began to wonder if he was the only one suffering from the loss of their closeness. He'd begun to depend on her and share things about his day with her. Now he couldn't. Now he was faced with yet another interview about what his favorite color was.

Jill was a sinking mass of confusion doing her best to stay afloat. The kava tea and ocean wave machine were not working their magic. To keep herself occupied, she accepted Trina's offer to lunch in the hospital cafeteria.

Making their way through the line, Jill took the grilled chicken Caesar salad, and Trina got a club sandwich. As soon as they sat down at a table, Trina made a moue of surprise. "Don't look now, but a reporter with an extremely questionable reputation is eating lunch with Dr. Logan."

Jill frowned even as her heart sped up. She hadn't seen him since she'd left his apartment. "Where is he?" she asked.

"Five o'clock, and I'm at twelve," Trina said. "That reporter is Danielle Crawford, and she is a menace."

Jill scanned the lunchtime crowd and immediately spotted Tyler. Her chest hurt in an odd way at the sight of him. She glanced at the woman with him who smiled, nodded and batted her eyes. The woman leaned forward and touched his arm. Jill felt her stomach tighten. Tyler was not hers, she reminded herself, and never would be. Strictly reining in her feelings, she turned her attention to her interest in him professionally. "Danielle Crawford? Questionable reputation? She isn't professional?"

Trina waved her hand. "Oh, she's probably fine as a reporter. She's just got a reputation as a man-eater. She's been married twice and engaged too many times to count." She looked in Tyler's direction. "Looks as if she'd like to eat Dr. Logan." She glanced back at Jill. "Aren't you going to do anything?"

Jill resisted the urge to look at Tyler. She picked at her salad instead. "Why should I do anything? If any man can handle himself with the ladies, Tyler can."

Trina's eyes grew wide. "But you two," she began. "I mean, it's common knowledge that the two of you are involved. At least, you have been until the last couple of days.''

Jill tightened her lips. ''Trina, my primary interest in Dr. Logan is in how he can best help accomplish his goal of getting the new wing. I'm sure you appreciate that,'' she said.

Trina wasn't one for subtlety. ''Sure you are, but Dr. Logan is so gorgeous any woman would jump at the chance to have him—''

''I'm not jumping,'' she told her assistant, who she had always thought might be better suited as a social secretary.

Trina glanced in Tyler's direction again. ''Well, I'll tell you one thing. If I had any—'' she paused and cleared her throat for effect ''—personal feelings for Dr. Logan, then seeing that woman put her hand on his knee would bring out the *me-ow* in *me*.''

The image of the attractive reporter touching him sent Jill's blood pressure zooming. She counted to ten, and chanted *Tyler is not mine.* ''Unless he needs my assistance in a professional way, it's none of my business. How is your club sandwich?''

Trina shot Jill a look of disbelief and shrugged. ''It's okay. What about your salad?''

Her nerves a mess, Jill put down her fork. ''It was delicious,'' she lied. ''But I'm full. Thank you for lunch, but I hope you'll excuse me. I need to get back to work.'' Jill returned her tray to the exit area, and on her way saw the reporter leaning forward and touching his arm. Surprised and dismayed at the strength of her reaction, she returned to her office, turned on her wave machine and paced.

This was just one of the reasons why she shouldn't have ever gotten intimately involved with Tyler, she told herself. She had always known he was a flirt and a babe magnet. The man would be a magnet for women when he was eighty, because he just knew how to remind a woman that she was female and make her glad of it. Zeroing in on just one woman would be difficult for him, she tried to tell herself, even though a part of her argued the point. She deliberately shut off her internal mental arguments and got to work.

Late that afternoon she paid a visit to Sam. "Hi, Sam," she said. "I brought you a new book."

"Jelly," he cried when he saw her, bouncing up and down. "Read to me! Sing oat song."

His reaction tugged at her heart. "You look like you're doing so much better. Are you still sore?"

Sam nodded, pointing to his chest. "Boo-boo," he said.

She carefully picked him up and sat in the rocker. "Well, you are going to be so much better soon. You'll be able to leave the hospital."

"At the end of the week, as a matter of fact," Tyler said from the doorway.

Jill's gaze tangled in his, while her heart seemed to stall.

"Hi, Doc," Sam said.

"Hi, boss," Tyler said, looking at the boy and grinning. He walked toward them and knelt down in front of the chair. "Let me take a look at your special boo-boo," he said.

"Do you want me to put him on the bed?" Jill asked.

"You can hold him. He looks happy where he is," Tyler said, his voice neutral, then turned to Sam. "You like Jelly holding you?"

Sam gave a big nod, but sat quietly while Tyler examined his stitches and listened to his heart. He reached for the bear on his stethoscope. "Bear."

Tyler looked at the boy thoughtfully. "You like him? His name is Cody. He might have a brother who will go with you when you leave the hospital. Would you like that?"

"Yeah. I don't have any brothers."

"You might with your new foster family," Tyler said, glancing at Jill. "Social Services will find a special-needs foster family to care for him while he's healing."

Jill hated the idea of Sam being bounced from one home to the next. "I'll visit you, too," she told Sam, who had stuck his finger in his mouth.

"Sing oat song, please," Sam said.

"Of course," she said, thinking there wasn't much she wouldn't do for this child. They'd been through such a dark time together and come out okay. Tyler, she recalled, had been there the whole way for both of them. Her feelings all over the spectrum, she sang the silly song, then read him the story of *The Velveteen Rabbit*.

"I thought you might like that story, since you like your rabbit so much," she said, too aware of Tyler's gaze on her.

Sam was busy looking at the pictures in the book.

"So, how did he win you over?" Tyler asked.

Caught off guard by the question, she shrugged. "I don't know. He just needed me," she said, searching his face for clues to his emotions, but Tyler seemed less open with her. She felt the inexplicable sting of loss. "Why?"

"Just curious," he said. "G'night, boss," he said to Sam.

"Night-night, Doc," Sam said. "Pet your bear?"

Tyler nodded and knelt down to let Sam pet the miniature bear. Jill tried not to love him for that. She tried with all her might, but it was such a tender thing for a busy, important doctor to do. How could she not love him for it?

Jill couldn't sleep. She hadn't slept well since she and Tyler had shared that awesome night together. At this rate she was going to wear out her sound machine. Not that it was doing her much good.

She glanced at the clock again when her doorbell rang just after midnight. Her adrenaline started humming. Besides the pizza and Chinese restaurant delivery guys, only one person rang her doorbell in Fort Worth.

She was reluctant to go to the door, but she had conversely missed him terribly. Rolling her eyes at her ambivalence, she checked the peephole and opened the door to Tyler. He stood, slightly disheveled, wearing his jeans and an irritated expression and carrying a duffel bag.

The duffel bag caused her some anxiety.

"I'm moving in," he told her.

Jill felt her jaw drop. "You're *what?*"

"Moving in," he said crisply as he strode past her. "*You* have made my life hell. My billboards might be bringing in the bucks for the hospital wing, but I'm not going to deal with the incessant calls from women. While you sat here in peace, my phone was ringing off the hook the entire evening. Dodging reporters' advances. I want protection," he told her, dumping his bag. "You are it."

His emotions swirled around her like a cyclone. "Protection? How can I be protection?"

"If I am living with you and appear to be involved with you, then I will be left alone," he told her.

Jill envisioned any chance for peace of mind slipping from her grasp. "But after I leave you'll have to deal with it."

"By then I'll be yesterday's news."

She felt a raging headache coming on. He would never be yesterday's news, but he had a point. She hated to admit it, but he had a point. "Don't you have a female friend or someone else who could help?''

''I haven't lived here that long,'' he told her. ''Besides you got me into this. You can get me out of it.''

''But, Tyler, given our—'' She broke off, searching for a description that wasn't emotionally charged. Something other than *mind-blowing, consuming, unforgettable night of making love.* ''—involvement,'' she said, ''don't you think this would be difficult?''

''Oh,'' he said. ''You mean because of the night you blew me away by making love with me and then the way you ran out on me the next morning?''

The hurt on his face was too difficult to bear. He made it seem as if she had been the callous one, when in her mind she had convinced herself her leaving wouldn't bother him. She remembered the tenderness he'd shown Sam and felt ashamed.

''I'm sorry,'' she said. ''Very sorry.''

His gaze searched hers. ''Why did you do that? How could you do that after that incredible night? It wasn't just about sex. It was about a joining of you totally with me.''

Her throat tightened and she swallowed hard. ''I know it was more than sex, although the sex was amazing,'' she said, her cheeks heating at the scorching memories. ''I was scared,'' she said. ''I am scared.''

''Of what?''

"Of how strongly I feel for you. It's new," she said.

"You didn't feel this way about your husband?"

She shook her head.

He moved closer, and she knew she was in trouble. "Then, you see," he said, lifting his hand to her cheek, "how rare this is. We can't let it pass by."

She resisted the urge to cradle her face in his palm. "But I'm not going to be here very long."

"All the more reason not to waste any time."

Craving his warmth, but still frightened, she closed her eyes. "I'm not sure I'm brave enough," she whispered.

"Jill, look at me," he said.

She warily met his gaze.

"I've watched you with Sam. You're the bravest woman I know."

"But Sam needs me."

"How do you know I don't need you?"

The room seemed to dip, and Jill was certain someone had moved the floor in her condo. "You are so strong, so self-sufficient—"

He covered her lips with his hand. "And so hungry for you. Don't waste the time we've got, Jill."

Jill felt herself sliding. She'd seen that expression of challenge and passion on his face before.

He slid his hand behind her nape and lowered his mouth to hers. "I dare you."

Ten

"That's not fair," Jill said.

"I'm playing to win," Tyler told her, rubbing his lips across hers. He would use any means to persuade her. The past few days had convinced him he couldn't miss her even if she was only here for a while. "What are you going to do?"

"Go crazy," she said, and put her arms around his neck. "Maybe I already have."

Tyler felt a wave of relief at her surrender. He didn't like how important she'd become to him, but denying it didn't change the fact. He pulled her against him and took her mouth as though he wanted to take all of her, thoroughly. He tasted her fear, but he also tasted her passion. She wanted him. The mere idea of it aroused him unbearably.

She pushed her fingers through his hair and moved restlessly against him. He could feel the budding tips of her nipples against her thin nightshirt and robe.

He could feel his desire clamoring for control. He wanted their clothes gone. He wanted her wrapped around him, taking him into her, enveloping him.

He pulled back slightly. "You have no idea how badly I wanted to kiss you when I saw you with Sam today."

Her gaze hazy with desire, but surprised, she stared at him curiously. "Why?"

"You're so tender with him."

"I felt the same way about you when you let him pet your miniature bear," she said, shaking her head in wonder. "I keep thinking you're too good to be true. You can't be real."

Her words were a balm to his sore heart. He took her mouth again and lifted his palm to cup her small breast. Her little gasp was like a stroke across his loins. He fought the urgency pushing him. "Let's go to bed," he said, trying to slow down.

"Later," she said, pulling his shirt free from his jeans and skimming her hands over his hardness. "I've missed you."

They didn't make it to bed until an hour later, and Tyler joined her in bed with his arm around her. She amazed him, what she did to him emotionally, intellectually, sexually. He felt an edgy reminder of the Logan Curse, but chased it away. Her even breaths reassured him. His last thought before he drifted off to sleep was that if she panicked again she couldn't leave this time. He was in her domain, and she would have a helluva time getting him out.

Tyler and Jill came to a mutual understanding. Since they could act crazy for each other during the time that Jill would stay in Forth Worth, they may as well go whole hog.

Jill poked gentle fun at him. She sent him pink roses at the hospital. Although he had difficulty explaining the mysterious gift to his colleagues, he was touched and amused. He returned the favor by bringing home Blue Bell ice cream, which he fed her nude, and, during the process, he somehow learned what the combination of her warm tongue and ice cream felt like on his body.

They made love frequently, with abandon, because they knew time was short. He joined her for some of her visits to Sam and fell a little harder for her each time he saw her with him.

On the other hand Jill felt as if she were walking a tightrope and she strongly suspected there was no net. She knew that, as high as she could climb with Tyler, as happy as she could be with him, when she left, her fall from glory could be devastating. When she was with him, he made it easy to forget everything was temporary.

The calendar on her desk, however, didn't fail to remind her, she thought as she put it facedown on her desk one afternoon.

A knock sounded at her office door.

Jill glanced at the sound in surprise. She so rarely heard a knock. Usually everyone just burst in unannounced.

She walked to the door and opened it to Clarence Gilmore. She smiled. That explained the knock. "Mr. Gilmore, how are you? Come in."

He nodded, entering and closing the door behind him. "Ms. Hershey, how are you today?"

She wondered at his fidgety movements. "Fine, and you?"

"Very fine, thank you. We are delighted with the results of your consultation with the hospital. You have performed beyond our wildest dreams," he said. "The target for the pediatric wing has been met and exceeded, and donations continue to come in." He put his hands in his pockets and removed them. "We really couldn't be more pleased."

"Thank you," she said, feeling a small surge of pleasure. "I'm glad I could help make it happen. I think Dr. Logan's willingness to participate was a huge bonus."

Clarence nodded. "Yes," he said, laughing uneasily. "Better him than me." He cleared his throat. "Now that we've exceeded our goal, we're in the unique position of telling you that if you need to leave us early for your next assignment, we'll understand."

An awkward silence followed. Jill shrugged.

"I'm sorry. I'm not sure I understand what you're saying."

"We do have a contract with you and your company, based on the number of weeks you work here. Of course, if you had needed to go over that time, we would have extended your salary. It probably isn't typical, but since you've finished early, we might be able to save the hospital a little money by releasing you from the contract early and wishing you well on your future endeavors."

Her stomach fell. Jill stared at him in surprise, although she supposed she shouldn't be surprised. Every time she had spoken with Clarence he had asked the question "How much?" She understood that was his job. Someone had to oversee the complicated financial matters of the hospital.

"It probably sounds as if I'm trying to kick you out, doesn't it?" Clarence asked, a miserable tone to his voice. "Ms. Hershey, if it were left to me, I would want you to stay on indefinitely. With your reputation, I was surprised we were able to get you in the first place. But we are not a huge facility, and we have to watch every penny. You are by no means obligated to leave before the end of your contract, but unfortunately I am obligated to offer you the option."

Clarence looked so downcast she felt sorry for him. Jill mustered a smile. "You're just doing what you're supposed to do. I'll think about what loose ends I need to tie up, and get back to you after the weekend.''

"Yes," Clarence said, slightly relieved. "And, Ms. Hershey, you truly have worked magic for us.''

Jill couldn't have felt less magical as she and Tyler prepared to make the trip to the Logan ranch for Brock and Felicity's wedding. She persuaded him to take her car instead of his motorcycle so they both could relax. On the way, she kept him busy with questions about every subject except the subject most on her mind—leaving Fort Worth.

"Do you miss the ranch when you're away?'' Jill asked.

"I do. Even though I know I was meant to practice medicine, a big part of me hates the city and longs for life on the ranch.''

"Maybe someday you could get a weekend place where you could escape.''

Tyler shook his head. "My brother would kill me. He still wants me there at roundup and any other chance I can manage it.''

"Do you resent it?''

"Are you kidding? After the way he went to bat for me with Dad, there's not much I wouldn't do for him. I think my dad had visions of all of us settling somewhere on the ranch and having tons of children and building some sort of Logan empire, but Brock's different, more practical. Don't get me wrong. He's got ranching in his blood, but—''

Jill felt the blood drain from her face. Hearing

Tyler talk of having children was a cutting reminder that she could never bear his children. She felt his glance and prayed her face didn't show her feelings.

"What's wrong?"

"Nothing," she said, and tried hard to smile. "I probably should have eaten more at lunch. Go ahead."

"Are you sure?"

"Yes! Go ahead."

Tyler looked unsettled, but he continued. "Brock is trying to take the best of the old ranching methods and the new ranching business views to keep the Logan ranch successful. He's got a tough job, and I admire him for his tenacity. I'm glad he's got Felicity."

"What happened to his first wife?"

"The Logan Curse," he said. His eye twitched, but he forced a laugh. "I'm joking. He just married the wrong girl. She wasn't cut out to live on a ranch. She had the kids, then left him for California."

Jill gasped. "But those kids are a treasure."

Tyler smiled at her outrage and lifted her hand to his mouth while he watched the road. "We think so."

"And Felicity?"

"As far as she's concerned, those kids are hers. She has wanted a family her whole life and she feels like she hit the jackpot."

"I would think with all that family," she began, "that you would want some of your own."

He shook his head. "I've already got plenty."

She searched his expression for clues. He looked thoughtful, almost brooding. She wondered if he was thinking about children or the Logan Curse. He dismissed it so easily, but every time he mentioned it, he seemed to grow tense.

Jill tugged on his hand. "Where are you?" she asked with a gentle smile.

"Right here," he said, but he still appeared distracted.

"Okay, then tell me what you were like when you were a teenager," she said.

"If I'd had the chance, I would have been wild as the March Hare, but my dad kept me busy to keep me out of trouble. I wanted a convertible." He shook his head at the memory. "No chance with my dad. It was a truck or nothing.

"I used to sneak out at night every now and then and drink beer with some friends. He caught me once and made me muck stalls for two months straight." He made a face. "Ruined my appreciation for beer.

"I wanted to sneak a girl into one of the barns and—"

"Something tells me you fulfilled this fantasy repeatedly," she said in a wry voice.

"There you go making assumptions again. I was shy with girls," he told her, and shot her a chiding look when she laughed. "I also got into a lot of fights with one of our neighbors—guy named Noah

Coltrane. He just couldn't seem to keep his mouth shut about the Logans, and I just couldn't seem to resist punching him for it. We both were sent home from school too many times to count.''

"This is the grudge neighbor,'' she said.

"Exactly. We share a stream with them and we can't fence that area, so that's been an ongoing source of conflict. Plus one of the Coltranes tried to steal one of the Logan brides a few generations back and was partially successful.'' Tyler nodded. "Yep, we've got a history of not getting along. At this point our best shot at peace is to pretend the other doesn't exist.''

Jill shook her head. "You get along well with so many people. It's hard for me to imagine you carrying a grudge with anyone.''

"Hate to admit it, but this one has been bred into me. There are people and things that can make me angry, though. A good example is the guy who got Martina pregnant. If Brock or I ever find out who isn't owning up to his responsibility, he'll wish the Texas Rangers were after him instead of the Logans.''

"That must be why Martina won't tell you who the father is.''

Tyler narrowed his eyes and frowned. "It makes me furious that someone took advantage of her. She may be a firecracker, but she's my little sister and I want to protect her.''

"Even if she doesn't think she needs your protection," she said, recalling the fact that his little sister was over five foot eight.

"Damn right," he said.

Jill smiled. "I haven't seen this protective, almost chauvinistic side of you."

He tossed her a sideways glance. "Stick around. You might be surprised," he said in a seductive voice.

Her stomach fluttered in response to his tone, but his invitation was a sad reminder that she wouldn't be sticking around and she wouldn't be learning all the sides that made up Tyler Logan.

The wedding took place the following afternoon outside on the ranch. The weather cooperated by supplying plenty of sunshine, and bluebells bloomed in abundance. Brock looked just a tad nervous as he stood in front of the guests with the minister and Tyler. Tyler kept catching Jill's gaze and simply staring at her. He was so overt about it people sitting next to her began to make comments.

"How long have you known Tyler?" a woman asked.

"Just a couple of months," Jill said, fighting the heat in her cheeks.

"It looks like he sure is interested in you. Will there be more Logan wedding bells?"

"No," Jill quickly said. "No more bells or weddings or anything of that nature."

She bared her teeth at Tyler and mouthed, "Stop looking at me."

When he still didn't look away, Jill focused on the rest of the wedding. The setup was simple but lovely. Chairs were lined up, the center aisle edged with colorful pots of flowers. At the front stood an archway dripping with greenery and flowers, and off to the side a classical guitarist played.

Dressed in their Sunday best, Bree and Jacob walked down the aisle, followed by Martina who cast a wink at Jill.

Felicity was radiant in a simple but exquisite white tea-length dress Grace Kelly could have worn. As Felicity walked down the aisle to meet Brock, Jill saw the way his gaze fastened on hers with so much love it almost hurt to watch.

The minister began the sweet ceremony. When he asked if there was any reason the two shouldn't join, Jacob tugged at his collar and piped up, "Sure ain't. We got her. Now we want to keep her."

A ripple of laughter swept over the guests, and Jill was surprised to feel tears form in her eyes. After all, she didn't know these people very well. Why should she be so moved? she wondered, and looked at Tyler. Perhaps it was her love for him that extended to anyone important to him. Yes, she'd realized she loved him, she just hadn't burdened him with that fact.

Aside from Tyler, though, Jill felt drawn to the Logans. She appreciated the fact that things hadn't always been easy for them, but they'd always hung together and done the hard work necessary to turn the bad times into good times. The love among them was so strong she envied it because she knew she would never truly be a part of them.

With strong voices, Felicity and Brock made their promises. The minister pronounced them man and wife, and Felicity appeared to reach up and tenderly wipe a tear from Brock's face.

The gesture brought more tears to Jill's eyes, and she watched Brock give his bride a long, soul-stirring kiss that had the whole crowd applauding.

At the reception a country music band played and guests dined at tables loaded with food. Tyler appeared by her side and put his arm around her. "We could do some two-stepping now."

His gaze held the same intent, sensual quality that always made her heart jump. "It'll be a little different from last time," she said, referring to the first night they'd made love.

His eyes darkened as he guided her to the dancing area and took her into his arms. "Unfortunately," he said. "I guess folks might get a little upset if I took off your dress."

She smiled at him and gave a little shake of her head as she followed his sliding steps. "You look very nice today. I haven't seen you in a suit since the very first time I met you."

"You were so impressed with me you decided to come down to Fort Worth," Tyler said.

"I thought you were cocky and pushy, and I still think you are," she said, feeling a sudden attack of longing. "I just wish I knew all the other things that you are."

"You will," he said, "in time."

"We don't have a lot of time." The words escaped her lips before she could stop them.

"What do you mean?"

Jill felt the weight of her discussion with Clarence heavy on her mind and conscience. "Just that my work is almost done," she told him. "And it will be time for me to go."

Tyler frowned. "I'm not ready for you to go."

The sting of tears in her eyes shocked her.

Tyler cupped her cheek and stopped dancing. "You're crying. What's going on?"

She blinked furiously. "This isn't the place or occasion," she told him, upset that she hadn't been able to hold her emotions in check. "We can talk about it another time."

"We can talk about it now," Tyler insisted.

Jill glanced around at the people regarding them curiously, then back at Tyler. "Later, after the reception. You need to focus on your brother. It's his wedding day."

"My brother's fine. If I know him, he'd just as soon leave the public party and start the private one right now. C'mon," he said, his gaze turbulent. "I know where to go."

In silence he guided her past the crowd of wedding guests, away from the music, down the lane to a barn. It was cool and dim inside. He urged her to sit on a bale of hay and stood in front of her, his hands on his hips.

Jill thought he must be the most incredible man she'd ever met and she could very well be leaving him within the week. The prospect cut at her.

"What is it?"

There was no use not telling him. He would get it out of her soon enough. She hated to spoil the happy occasion with her news. "It's a good news, bad news situation. The good news," she told him, "is that we've already raised more than enough money for your wing."

"That's great," he said, a grin splitting his face. "What could be bad about that?"

"Well, Clarence came to see me in my office Friday afternoon. I thought I was going to be here another month, but he said since we accomplished everything ahead of schedule, I could go ahead and leave."

Tyler's grin fell.

Feeling her throat tighten with emotion, she swallowed hard. "We always knew I would be leaving. We both talked about it, and I knew I would leave, but I just didn't expect—" Her voice broke, not allowing her to finish. She found little comfort in the pained expression on his face.

He shook his head. "I'm going to kill Clarence."

Jill laughed through her tears. "It's not his fault.

He's doing his job. He's just trying to save the hospital some money.''

He set his jaw. ''I'm going to fix this.''

''You can't fix this. We both know I have to leave sometime.''

''It doesn't have to be now.''

Jill didn't want to argue about it. She didn't want to think about it anymore. She wouldn't be able to be a part of many of Tyler's dreams and wishes, but she could feel good about helping make the wing a reality. Out of the blue she suddenly remembered what Tyler had said about wanting to make love in a barn. Maybe she could make another wish come true.

Eleven

"**I**'m surprised at you," Jill said, tugging at his tie for him to move closer to her.

He frowned. "Why are you surprised? You didn't think I'd be pleased to hear you're leaving, did you?"

"No," she said, standing and looking at him with a smile full of feminine invitation. "I'm just surprised at you." She slowly skimmed her finger down his chest to the top of his slacks. "You've been waiting for this opportunity for over ten years and you're not doing a thing about it."

"What opportunity?" he asked, allowing her to distract him just for the moment.

She shrugged, and the movement of her breasts

distracted him further. "I thought you told me you'd been wanting to sneak a girl into the barn for years. Is talking all you wanted to do?" she asked in a sexual taunt that might as well have been an intimate caress.

It took two seconds for her implication to sink in. It took no time for him to decide to take her up on her offer. Maybe the wedding had made him a little crazy, but he'd felt extraordinarily possessive of Jill the entire day. He wanted to take her, to make her his, in an unmistakable, basic way. "You never cease to amaze me," he muttered and pulled her against him and slid her zipper down.

Her dress fell to her feet in a pool of silk. Her breasts were small ivory mounds jutting from her bra of lace. Tyler knew her body well enough to see the sexy sign of arousal, her stiff nipples. He lowered his mouth to nudge her bra down and roll his tongue over the sensitive tip. He knew her soft intake of breath and the restless rubbing of her thighs together meant she was wet and wanting him.

He could imagine taking her a hundred different ways, and he wanted to do each one all at once. With his fingers, he sought the sweet secret between her thighs at the same time he kissed her. Her hands wandered restlessly over his shoulders and down his back. She felt a little wild in his arms, as if she, too, couldn't get enough of him. The knowledge made him want to plunge inside her immediately.

She pulled her mouth from his, her lips already

swollen from his kiss, her eyes already hazy with passion. "You always make me so crazy I forget what I want to do," she accused him.

"Is that bad?" he asked, reaching for her again.

She shook her head. "No, but this time it's my turn to lead the two-step." She unfastened his slacks, slid down his zipper and enveloped him with her hand.

He groaned. "What do you have in mind?"

She gave him a French kiss that blew his mind, then flowed down his body like a warm, sultry breeze. Her breath drifted over his aching hardness. She looked up at him and kissed him intimately.

Tyler swore. The sight was too erotic for words. Jill, with her bare breasts brushing his thighs and her gorgeous, sassy lips on him. She tasted and taunted him with her tongue, then enveloped him with her soft velvet mouth milking his response. He couldn't last. Between her bold seduction and his need, emotional and sexual, for her, he felt as if he were going to explode.

He cupped his hand under her jaw and massaged her cheeks. "You're pushing me out of control. I want inside," he told her in a voice dark and husky to his own ears.

Grabbing a blanket, he sat on the ground and pulled her on top. She gazed at him in sensual surprise, then straddling him, she eased down on him. Guiding her, he thrust, and she rode him stroke by incredible stroke until she clenched around him and he went straight over the edge.

She sank down on him, tucking her face in his shoulder. "When you think of sneaking a girl into the barn," she told him, "I hope you'll always think of me." She took a deep breath and whispered, "I love you."

His heart twisted. For one moment he wanted to know how forever with her might feel. For one moment he thought about having a family with Jill. He thought of babies and laughter and love. And loss. He frowned, wondering why he always paired marriage with loss in his mind. It couldn't be the curse, he thought. After all his denying and rationalizing, he didn't really believe in that foolishness, did he?

He couldn't, he thought, and held her tightly.

"We should get back to the reception," Jill said. "Your brother will wonder where you are."

"He may wonder, but he'll never dream what you've been doing to me," Tyler said and grinned.

"What *I've* been doing to *you*," she said, her hair tousled and her eyes still blurry with her passion for him. "How about what *you* have been doing to *me?*"

He kissed her protests away. "How about what we've been doing to each other? Better?"

She nodded, and he helped pull her and himself together. Just as they were leaving the barn, she said, "I meant what I said. When you think of taking a girl to a barn, think of me and smile."

I'll think of you whenever I think of the woman who fills me up and makes me crazy, he thought.

"I will," he simply promised, and resolved to speak to Clarence Gilmore.

As they returned to the reception, he squeezed her arm. "I'll get your punch and check in with Brock," he told her. "That's what I'd been about to do before we left."

"Thanks," she said.

Tyler grabbed some punch and nodded to Brock who was watching an elderly neighbor dance with Felicity. "You've done it now," Tyler said. "How does it feel to be completely tied up?"

"I want her tied to me," Brock said. "I'll be glad when this reception is over. Seems to me the men are using it as an excuse to dance with Felicity. A few more minutes, and I'm calling a halt to it. Enough's enough," he said emphatically. He glanced at Tyler. "Where'd you go for so long?"

Tyler shrugged. "Just needed to talk with Jill in private."

Brock gave a slow smile. "Did you ask her to marry you?"

Tyler felt the claw of panic. "Hell, no! We were talking about when she's scheduled to finish the project at the hospital and leave Fort Worth." Speaking the words wrenched at him.

Brock looked at him in disbelief. "You're gonna let her go?"

Tyler shrugged. "She has to go back sometime,

but it won't be soon,'' he said. ''I'll make sure of that.''

Brock raised an eyebrow. ''Don't let the Logan Curse keep you from the right woman,'' he said.

Tyler's eye twitched. ''I don't believe in the Logan Curse, remember?'' he asked rhetorically, but he didn't sound convinced to his own ears.

''It takes finding the right woman to break—''

Just then, a man on horseback thundered across a field toward the wedding reception. ''What the hell—'' Tyler began, squinting his eyes to identify the man.

''Horse looks like a Coltrane's,'' Brock muttered. ''They always did have an eye for nice horseflesh.''

''It's Noah,'' Tyler said.

''How can you tell from here?'' Brock asked.

''We beat each other up so much I'd know him if I ran into him in the dark in Canada.'' He gestured for Jill to join him. He wanted her next to him. No telling what a Coltrane would do.

Brock swore and went after Felicity.

Jill quickly joined Tyler. ''Who is it?''

''Noah Coltrane.''

Her eyes widened. ''Oh.''

Noah slowed the stallion and guided the impressive animal right up to the dance area, which had been vacated as the guests watched in amazement. He appeared to scan the area.

Tyler spoke up. ''What do you want, Noah?''

Noah, a man with coal-black eyes, met his gaze. "I'm here to see Martina."

A collective gasp swept over the guests.

Click, click, click. Tyler quickly added up his sister's pregnancy and Noah Coltrane's presence, and rage rolled through him. "I'm gonna kill him."

Jill grabbed his suit coat. "No, you're not."

Tyler watched Felicity step in front of Brock.

"She doesn't want to see you," Tyler called to him, shaking loose from Jill's grasp. "Get off the property. Can't you see we're having a wedding?"

"That means she's here," Noah said, surveying the crowd once again.

"Buy a vowel," Tyler said. "She doesn't want to see you."

He saw a hint of desperation come and go in the man's eyes and felt a startling identification with it. He'd seen that same expression in Brock's eyes and felt it in his own gut. About Jill. He swore under his breath, fighting a multitude of strange emotions.

Noah's face hardened. "I will see her," he said. "Give her that message."

With that he thundered off. Tyler exchanged a glance with Brock. He couldn't believe what his sister had done. There had to be a terrific explanation for this, he thought, and he was going to hear it shortly.

The wedding guests soon left, probably to share the tale with their neighbors. Good gossip was sometimes difficult to find in this part of West Texas.

Tyler took Jill's hand and joined Brock and Felicity on the quick trek back to the house to find Martina. The housekeeper watched over Bree and Jacob while the catering crew began the cleanup.

After an excruciating three minutes of silence, Jill broke it. "You look beautiful, Felicity. I don't think I've seen a more radiant bride."

Felicity gave a small smile. "Thank you. I'm truly glad you could come."

Jill detected a mile-wide note of concern in the bride's voice. "She must really feel stuck between a rock and a hard place."

"Who?" Tyler asked, but everyone knew who—Martina.

"Your sister," she said. "She obviously loves you two and is devoted to her family, but she's carrying the baby of someone you hate."

"When do you think it happened?" Brock asked Tyler.

"Chicago," Tyler said decisively.

"Maybe she got hit on the head."

"Or fell in love," Felicity and Jill said at the same time.

"Never," Brock said.

"When hell freezes over," Tyler said.

Jill just sighed as they climbed the stairs to the house. "Watch out for icicles."

Martina was carrying her suitcase downstairs. Despite Martina's fire, Jill felt a great deal of sympathy for her.

Martina caught sight of her brothers and gave a sigh. "Well, I guess you figured out the stork didn't do it."

"How did it happen?" Brock demanded.

She winced. "That's a little personal."

Tyler shook his head. "How could you?"

Vulnerability shadowed her eyes. "I didn't plan to get pregnant," she said. "I didn't plan to get involved."

"But with a Coltrane?" Brock said in distaste.

"In the beginning he wasn't what I'd thought he would be," she said, her gaze growing sad. "I made a mistake, but the baby won't be one," she said with determination. "If you can't accept it, tell me now and I'll never come around again."

Another awful silence followed where Brock and Tyler clearly tried to digest the news. Jill tensed at the expressions on their faces.

Felicity stepped forward and embraced Martina. "Of course we'll accept your baby. Your brothers love you. How could they not love your child?"

"Be angry and yell later," Jill whispered to Tyler. "She needs you now."

Tyler stepped forward and took his sister in his arms. "I may never understand this," he told her. "But there's nothing you could do to keep me from loving you and worrying about you. I'd protect you with my life,'' he said. ''We'll do the same for your baby.''

Martina's eyes filled with tears. ''I was so afraid you would hate me.''

''Never,'' Brock said, taking his turn at holding her.

Jill watched Tyler struggle with his own emotions. He crammed his hands in his pockets. ''What are you going to do?''

''Leave,'' Martina said simply.

''I told him you didn't want to see him.''

''You told him right.''

''If he's the father,'' Brock warned, ''you'll have to deal with his rights sometime.''

''Not now,'' Martina said, her face closed.

Tyler sighed. ''I'll carry your bag to the car,'' he said, and Brock joined him.

Martina turned to Felicity. ''I'm sorry this ruined your wedding.''

Felicity shook her head. ''It didn't ruin it. I still got your brother,'' she said with a smile. ''It just added a little drama. Brock was getting tired of the reception, anyway.''

Martina gave a small smile and hugged her. ''I'm glad he found you.''

She looked at Jill. ''If you love Tyler, you need to realize that he's scared spitless of getting married. He'll deny it to his dying day, but he's scared of losing. It will take a strong woman to break through that, but it will be worth it.''

Jill suffered with the fact that she would be leaving him soon. "He is a very special man," she said quietly.

Martina nodded in approval. "Yes, he is." She swiped at her eyes. "I should go."

Jill hated seeing the loneliness in her eyes. "You could come to Fort Worth."

Martina shook her head. "No, I'll head back to Dallas. It'll be a while before I come here again," she told Felicity.

"I wish you wouldn't say that," Felicity said.

Unable to let her leave without some offer of assistance, Jill pulled a card from her purse. "I'm not your brother or even a Logan, but I hate the idea of you being pregnant and alone. If you need anything," Jill said, "or need to get away from Texas for a little bit, please know you can call me."

Martina took her card and nodded. "Thanks. You never know, I might decide a trip to D.C. would be a great idea. Y'all take care."

Jill watched her descend the steps and embrace her brothers, then she was gone. When Brock and Tyler returned to the house, Felicity tugged her new husband upstairs for a few moments of privacy.

Tyler turned to Jill. "Thanks for keeping me from doing something stupid."

"Punching Noah Coltrane?"

He shook his head. "That would have been satisfying. Letting Martina leave without knowing we wouldn't stop loving her would have been a big mistake. I'm still upset as hell, but she's got the bigger problem and she doesn't need Brock and me loading her up with our grudge with the Coltranes.''

She touched his arm. ''That's extremely clear-headed considering you probably wanted to tar and feather him.''

He looked down at her thoughtfully. ''Having you here made a difference for me.''

Jill's chest tightened as she remembered Martina's words. How could Jill be the strong woman he needed when she felt so vulnerable? How could she be there for him when she was leaving? She tried to push her thoughts aside. The day had been so full she could barely make sense of it all, and Jill suspected her private turmoil was just beginning.

After saying goodbye, Jill and Tyler left that evening for Fort Worth. Everyone at the Logan Ranch seemed to need some breathing space from the festivities and Martina's revelation. Jill wondered if that was the last time she would see Brock and Felicity, but she tried not to dwell on it. She insisted on driving during the return trip, and Tyler was silent most of the way.

That night in bed, they just held each other. It was a sweet comfort to her soul to have him in her arms.

On Monday she struggled with her indecision of when to leave but began the process of turning over the heart menders' project to the on-site PR coordinator. Tyler popped in to see her several times.

Trina stood beside her, sighing. "You're so lucky," she said. "He's everything a woman could want—good-looking, a doctor, interesting, sexy." She shook her head. "And you know he's going to be a great father. He was *born* to be a father. This is a man who should definitely be reproduced."

This is a man who should definitely by reproduced.

Trina left her office, and Jill stood stock-still as Trina's words rocked through her and exploded. The pain was overwhelming in its intensity. Truth, she thought. If ever something was true, this was it. For all his talk about not wanting a family, his roots would eventually lead him to create his own personal legacy. Tyler would make a great father. He should have children. She couldn't make that happen for him.

In all her confusion about how and when to leave, she had never considered the monumental truth. She knew him intimately and knew even better than Trina that he should indeed be reproduced.

Nausea rose in her throat. How could she have been so blind? She wrapped her arms around her waist, comforting herself at the thought of what she would have to do. Before she'd been uncertain, but now it was crystal clear what she must do.

Twelve

When Jill made love with Tyler that night, she tried to love him with enough tenderness and passion to last a lifetime for herself and him. With every touch and every stroke, she tried to convey her love, to love him enough on the outside that he could feel it on the inside.

When morning dawned, however, she knew that sometime that day she would have to tell him she was leaving. She spent the day making airline arrangements, tying up loose ends and visiting Sam. In the midst of the loss of her relationship with Tyler, Jill realized that for herself she could still share her love with a child even if she hadn't given birth to him. She called the Social Services representative and discussed the possibility of adopting Sam.

By the end of the workday, she was exhausted but resolved. Tyler was working the night shift, and he had told her he would come see her before he made rounds. He swung into her office with a sexy grin and immediately took her into his arms. "I must be getting old. You wore me out last night."

She took a tiny breath. Her tight chest would only allow that much.

He pulled back. "I'm not complaining." He looked at her thoughtfully. "What's up?"

Jill looked away from him. She didn't know how to tell him. She only knew she must.

"I'm leaving tomorrow."

Silence followed.

"You can't."

Jill heard a little of his heart hurting in his tone, and she nearly broke down. Heaven help her. She walked behind her desk, hoping the barrier would keep her emotions from tumbling out. "Yes, I am." She bit her lip. "We both knew I would leave. Clarence has asked me to leave."

"Clarence can unask you," Tyler yelled.

His volume snapped her head back. She met his gaze, and the pain she saw in his eyes made her pray she was doing the right thing. "Tyler, we both knew I would leave. It's not just that I live in Washington, D.C., and you live here. Neither of us wanted to make a permanent commitment to each other, anyway, so dragging it out is just going to make it more difficult for you or for me to get on with our lives."

"Is it that easy for you to just cut it off and leave?" he demanded angrily.

"No, it's not. But I'm not the right woman for you. Someday you're going to decide to settle down." She lifted her hand when he opened his mouth to protest. "Just listen. Someday you're going to decide you want to have children. And you should," she said, feeling her eyes fill with tears. "You should, because you will be an awesome father. Your children will be so lucky to have you as their father. I can't give you babies." The words spoken from her mouth sliced her to ribbons. "I lost the ability to have children. Someday you're going to want those babies, and I love you too much to take that away from you."

Tyler looked shell-shocked. "You can't have children."

Jill shook her head. "That's right. I can't."

Emotions warred for dominion on his face. Confusion, pain, frustration. He strode in front of her desk. "We won't need to deal with children now, Jill. This is about us, you and me, now."

"We can't just deal with you and me now," she said. "We have to deal with you and me past and you and me future. I love you and I refuse to take something this important from your future. Besides," she reminded him, "you didn't want to make a commitment to me."

His pager went off. He swore and pointed his finger at her emphatically. His gaze burned holes in her heart. "I have to go, but if you really love me, you will not leave."

He was gone like the wind, and with her tears falling like rain, she whispered to his back, "If I really love you, then I'll leave."

Two surgeries in one night and Jill announcing her impending departure. It was 7:00 a.m. and Tyler felt like an old man. He called her condo, but there was no answer. He wondered if she was avoiding him.

Letting himself into her office, he went in and sat down in her chair behind the desk to wait for her. More than anything, he wanted to feel her presence. If he concentrated hard enough, he could almost smell her soft, floral scent.

Tyler propped his arms on her desk and sank his head into his hands. He'd found a woman who rocked his world, and now she was going to leave it. He had no idea how to keep her. His sense of humor, charm and medical degree were not going to help him now.

Something about her made him want to be the best he could be, yet at the same time he could count on her support when he didn't meet his standards. He didn't want to go the rest of his life without that. Hell, he didn't want to go five minutes.

Had it finally happened to him? Had he finally met *the* woman? He didn't doubt for one minute that he wanted to spend now and forever with her. He'd been so busy avoiding the idea of commitment that he hadn't listened to his heart.

Heaven knows the Logans had gotten into trouble when they listened to their hearts. The threat of the Logan Curse mocked him. "Don't fall in love, because you will lose."

A disturbing idea settled in his gut. In this case was it a self-fulfilling prophecy? Had he chosen someone who would leave? He shook his head at the thought. He'd watched Jill in her trial by fire. That was a woman who could stick through the worst.

Tyler wondered if he had made it easy for her to leave. No strings, no commitment, no future plans. Easy, he thought, his earlier attitude damning him.

He played a game of what-if.

"What if I'm in love with her?" He said the words aloud to see if they were real. "I am," he said, the realization both freeing and painful.

"What if I want to marry her?

"I do," he said, amazed at how easily the truth came when he wasn't fighting it.

"What about kids?"

Tyler stared into the darkness and mourned the loss of Jill's ability to have children. He would have loved to make her big with his child. But it was more important to him to have her in his life.

The door whooshed open and he looked up, hoping to see Jill. It was Trina. His heart fell.

"Dr. Logan," she said awkwardly. "I didn't expect you to be here. I just thought I'd do one more pass over for Jill in case she left something." She sighed. "She did a great job, but it's sad that she had to leave. I bet you're going to miss her."

Tyler frowned. "When is she stopping by today?"

Trina shook her head. "Oh, she's not coming in today. She's got a morning flight."

"Morning flight?" he thundered, standing. "When?"

Trina blinked. "I think around ten o'clock."

"Flight 534 for Washington, D.C., now boarding passengers seated in rows five through thirty."

Jill ignored the lump in her throat and gathered her carry-on bag. "That's me," she murmured to herself, surprised her heart had not been ripped from her chest. Surely it couldn't be hurting this badly and still beating.

I'm doing the right thing. I'm doing the right thing, she chanted to herself again. She'd been chanting it nearly nonstop during her endless, sleepless night and endless drive to the Dallas/Fort Worth airport.

"I'm doing the right thing," she whispered.

"No, you're not."

Jill slowed at the sound of Tyler's voice. For a moment she wondered if she'd imagined it. Lack of sleep did that to people, didn't it?

"I love you."

Jill stopped at the sound of his voice at her back. She *must* be dreaming, she thought, but turned around.

Tyler stood there in his medical coat, his hair mussed, circles under his blue, anxious eyes. Jill could only gape at him.

"I'm not here to see you off," he told her with

no smile in sight, and got down on one knee. "Marry me."

The floor tilted, the entire airport spun. She stared at him, feeling her body begin to tremble, starting with her feet.

"I want to be with you forever," he said. "You make me want to know how forever feels. Marry me, Jill."

Her head was swimming. "But I thought you didn't want commitment."

"I was so used to saying I didn't want to get married, I couldn't hear myself when I really wanted to," he told her. "And about children," he said, his expression serious, "I will have hundreds of children through my career. I can only have one you."

Tears began to fall down her cheeks. She sniffed and swiped at her damp face. "Oh, Tyler are you sure?"

"Lady, he'd better be sure," a bystander cracked. "He's got witnesses." It suddenly occurred to Jill that they had an audience. Jill had only had eyes for Tyler. She tugged his hand, urging him to stand. "Get up."

"I'm double parked. I'm pretty sure my bike has been towed, so I hope you'll give me a ride home. You haven't answered me," he said, keeping hold of her hand at the announcement for final boarding.

"Where is home?" she asked, still unable to believe. She'd had no hope.

"Wherever we are together. Jill, stop torturing me. Will you marry me?"

"Can we adopt Sam?"

His gaze was unbearably tender. "Yes."

"I will marry you, Tyler Logan," she promised, barely noticing a scattered applause as Tyler took her into his arms. "What about the Logan Curse?" she whispered, her heart overflowing.

"From the very beginning I told you that you were a sorceress. You worked your magic and broke it."

"I'm not magic," she protested.

He shook his head, the love in his eyes brighter than the sun and bigger than Texas. "You are, for me."

*   *   *   *   *

Watch for Martina Logan's story in

EXPECTING HIS CHILD

*The final book in Leanne Banks's
exciting miniseries*

LONE STAR FAMILIES: THE LOGANS

*On sale in May from Silhouette Desire
And now for a sneak preview of*

EXPECTING HIS CHILD,

please turn the page.

Prologue

He thundered across the dusty Texas soil on the back of a black stallion looking like an avenging angel. Panic flooded her bloodstream. Martina Logan quickly backed away from the crowd of wedding guests and hid behind a tree. The guests at her brother's outdoor wedding gasped and murmured. Not many would be able to identify him from this distance, but Martina could. Her eyes didn't need to tell her; her heart did the trick, pounding erratically against her rib cage.

Noah Coltrane.

Noah slowed the stallion and guided the impressive animal to the vacated dance area. He scanned the crowd and Martina tried to make herself shrink.

Her brother Tyler spoke up. "What do you want, Noah?"

"I'm here to see Martina."

Her stomach dipped to her knees and she prayed he wouldn't see her. She wasn't ready to face him. Not yet.

"She doesn't want to see you," Tyler said. "Get off the property. Can't you see we're having a wedding?"

"That means she's here," Noah said, surveying the crowd once again.

"Buy a vowel," Tyler said. "She doesn't want to see you."

Martina closed her eyes during the long pause that followed.

"I will see her," Noah finally said, the hard resolve in his voice giving her a chill. "Give her that message."

Trembling, Martina allowed herself a moment of weakness and covered her face with her hands. A dozen images raced through her mind. Months ago, hearing Noah's Texas drawl on the stalled El in Chicago had reminded her how far from home she was. Hearing his voice had rubbed at an empty spot, and she had turned around to see the most fascinating man she had ever met.

Noah was not the usual cowboy. Not only did he rope and ride, he also fenced and traded cattle options on the Chicago exchange. When they'd met, Martina had been temporarily assigned to a computer company in the Windy City while Noah was taking a course in commodities. He'd charmed her and made her feel comfortable before revealing his name.

Martina still remembered the regret she'd felt and seen echoed on his face when they'd realized their families hated each other. There was enough bad blood between the two families to fill the Red Sea.

Still, Noah had suggested with a wry chuckle that since they weren't in Texas, they could pretend their last names were different.

He was the biggest no-no that she'd said yes to. It had been all too easy to fall for him, and the memory of the passion and laughter they'd shared still made her weak. But reality and family loyalty had eventually crept in. Their affair had ended as quickly as it had begun. Martina, however, had been left with the consequences of her temporary insanity called Noah Coltrane.

Martina bit her lip and opened her eyes. She touched her abdomen swollen with Noah's child. She dreaded the day she would have to face him. She knew it was coming. Noah Coltrane would always be her biggest no-no. Her favorite mistake.

If you enjoyed what you just read,
then we've got an offer you can't resist!

Take 2 bestselling
love stories FREE!

Plus get a FREE surprise gift!

Look Who's Celebrating Our 20th Anniversary:

"Silhouette Desire is the purest form of contemporary romance."
—*New York Times* bestselling author
Elizabeth Lowell

"Let's raise a glass to Silhouette and all the great books and talented authors they've introduced over the past twenty years. May the *next* twenty be just as exciting and just as innovative!"
—*New York Times* bestselling author
Linda Lael Miller

"You've given us a sounding board, a place where, as readers, we can be entertained, and as writers, an opportunity to share our stories.... You deserve a special round of applause on...your twentieth birthday. Here's wishing you many, many more."
—International bestselling author
Annette Broadrick

SILHOUETTE'S 20ᵀᴴ ANNIVERSARY CONTEST
OFFICIAL RULES
NO PURCHASE NECESSARY TO ENTER

1. To enter, follow directions published in the offer to which you are responding. Contest begins 1/1/00 and ends on 8/24/00 (the "Promotion Period"). Method of entry may vary. Mailed entries must be postmarked by 8/24/00, and received by 8/31/00.

2. During the Promotion Period, the Contest may be presented via the Internet. Entry via the Internet may be restricted to residents of certain geographic areas that are disclosed on the Web site. To enter via the Internet, if you are a resident of a geographic area in which Internet entry is permissible, follow the directions displayed on-line, including typing your essay of 100 words or fewer telling us "Where In The World Your Love Will Come Alive." On-line entries must be received by 11:59 p.m. Eastern Standard time on 8/24/00. Limit one e-mail entry per person, household and e-mail address per day, per presentation. If you are a resident of a geographic area in which entry via the Internet is permissible, you may, in lieu of submitting an entry on-line, enter by mail, by hand-printing your name, address, telephone number and contest number/name on an 8"x 11" plain piece of paper and telling us in 100 words or fewer "Where In The World Your Love Will Come Alive," and mailing via first-class mail to: Silhouette 20ᵗʰ Anniversary Contest, (in the U.S.) P.O. Box 9069, Buffalo, NY 14269-9069; (In Canada) P.O. Box 637, Fort Erie, Ontario, Canada L2A 5X3. Limit one 8"x 11" mailed entry per person, household and e-mail address per day. On-line and/or 8"x 11" mailed entries received from persons residing in geographic areas in which Internet entry is not permissible will be disqualified. No liability is assumed for lost, late, incomplete, inaccurate, nondelivered or misdirected mail, or misdirected e-mail, for technical, hardware or software failures of any kind, lost or unavailable network connection, or failed, incomplete, garbled or delayed computer transmission or any human error which may occur in the receipt or processing of the entries in the contest.

3. Essays will be judged by a panel of members of the Silhouette editorial and marketing staff based on the following criteria:

    Sincerity (believability, credibility)—50%

    Originality (freshness, creativity)—30%

    Aptness (appropriateness to contest ideas)—20%

    Purchase or acceptance of a product offer does not improve your chances of winning. In the event of a tie, duplicate prizes will be awarded.

4. All entries become the property of Harlequin Enterprises Ltd., and will not be returned. Winner will be determined no later than 10/31/00 and will be notified by mail. Grand Prize winner will be required to sign and return Affidavit of Eligibility within 15 days of receipt of notification. Noncompliance within the time period may result in disqualification and an alternative winner may be selected. All municipal, provincial, federal, state and local laws and regulations apply. Contest open only to residents of the U.S. and Canada who are 18 years of age or older, and is void where prohibited by law. Internet entry is restricted solely to residents of those geographical areas in which Internet entry is permissible. Employees of Torstar Corp., their affiliates, agents and members of their immediate families are not eligible. Taxes on the prizes are the sole responsibility of winners. Entry and acceptance of any prize offered constitutes permission to use winner's name, photograph and/or other likeness for the purposes of advertising, trade and promotion on behalf of Torstar Corp. without further compensation to the winner, unless prohibited by law. Torstar Corp and D.L. Blair, Inc., their parents, affiliates and subsidiaries, are not responsible for errors in printing or electronic presentation of contest or entries. In the event of printing or other errors which may result in unintended prize values or duplication of prizes, all affected contest materials or entries shall be null and void. If for any reason the Internet portion of the contest is not capable of running as planned, including infection by computer virus, bugs, tampering, unauthorized intervention, fraud, technical failures, or any other causes beyond the control of Torstar Corp. which corrupt or affect the administration, secrecy, fairness, integrity or proper conduct of the contest, Torstar Corp. reserves the right, at its sole discretion, to disqualify any individual who tampers with the entry process and to cancel, terminate, modify or suspend the contest or the Internet portion thereof. In the event of a dispute regarding an on-line entry, the entry will be deemed submitted by the authorized holder of the e-mail account submitted at the time of entry. Authorized account holder is defined as the natural person who is assigned to an e-mail address by an Internet access provider, on-line service provider or other organization that is responsible for arranging e-mail address for the domain associated with the submitted e-mail address.

5. Prizes: Grand Prize—a $10,000 vacation to anywhere in the world. Travelers (at least one must be 18 years of age or older) or parent or guardian if one traveler is a minor, must sign and return a Release of Liability prior to departure. Travel must be completed by December 31, 2001, and is subject to space and accommodations availability. Two hundred (200) Second Prizes—a two-book limited edition autographed collector set from one of the Silhouette Anniversary authors: Nora Roberts, Diana Palmer, Linda Howard or Annette Broadrick (value $10.00 each set). All prizes are valued in U.S. dollars.

6. For a list of winners (available after 10/31/00), send a self-addressed, stamped envelope to: Harlequin Silhouette 20ᵗʰ Anniversary Winners, P.O. Box 4200, Blair, NE 68009-4200.

Contest sponsored by Torstar Corp., P.O. Box 9042, Buffalo, NY 14269-9042.

ENTER FOR
A CHANCE TO WIN*
Silhouette's 20th Anniversary Contest

Tell Us Where in the World
You Would Like *Your* Love To Come Alive...
And We'll Send the Lucky Winner There!

Silhouette wants to take you wherever
your happy ending can come true.

Here's how to enter: Tell us, in 100 words or less,
where you want to go to make your love come alive!

In addition to the grand prize, there will be 200
runner-up prizes, collector's-edition book sets
autographed by one of the Silhouette anniversary
authors: **Nora Roberts, Diana Palmer,
Linda Howard** or **Annette Broadrick**.

DON'T MISS YOUR CHANCE TO WIN!
ENTER NOW! No Purchase Necessary

Silhouette®
Where love comes alive™

Name: _____

Address: _____

City: _____ State/Province: _____

Zip/Postal Code: _____

Mail to Harlequin Books: **In the U.S.**: P.O. Box 9069, Buffalo, NY
14269-9069; **In Canada**: P.O. Box 637, Fort Erie, Ontario, L4A 5X3